Behind Every Smile Lies a Broken Heart

DELORES O' DELANEY

Delaney Publishing

Delaney Publishing

ISBN: 978-0-578-20845-9

Cover Image by Delores O' Delaney

PRINTED IN THE UNITED STATES OF AMERICA

CONTENTS

ABOUT THE AUTHOR

I have always had the desire to write stories and allow readers to take a walk through my mind as I try to captivate their attention on how so many people have been struggling with the ability to over come different types of abuses. I hope this book will enlightened you on how to over come them.

DEDICATION

I truly like to give a special thanks to my husband, Kevin Price, who sat up every night with me as I read him chapter after chapter of my book. He has given me his true advice and always keeping it real with me, never once has he judge me for my past. My two children Castelle Ebo & Ka'vonna Price whom I've told in advance about my mistakes I've made in my life , yet they still love me. I want to give a special thanks to my cousin Mia Lyons, Annie Lyons & Rosa Lee Norfleet, may they rest in peace for continuing to push me to write my story. I would like to thank a host of family and friends. There are too many to name, but you know who you are and most of all I want to thank my lord and savior Jesus Christ.

Chapter 1

OUR BEAUTIFUL FAMILY

My mother's children are as follows: Chuck, Quay, Sherry and I (Katrina) all have the same father. My sister Tina has her own father. My sister tee-tee has her own father. Leroy, Rachel, and Denay have the same father who happens to live with us. His name is William . He treats us all the same. We were all his children in his eyes. He took the place of my birth father, Cedric. My mother's name is Cindy. We lived on the second floor apt 202, of building 2309 in North Philadelphia.

It was a Christmas morning Bill woke us up for a big breakfast. We gathered around the table filled with excitement. As we ate breakfast and drink hot coco. Some of us could hardly eat all of our food because we knew that we had toys under the tree waiting to be found by us.

William was a good man. We all received new clothes, baby dolls, trucks, coloring books, shoes and sneakers. We all loved him, even my evil big sister, Sherry, she didn't like anybody! After playing with our toys we got dressed and went outside to play in the snow in front our apartment building with our friends.

Mommy said it was ok to go outside, but we were to stay where she could see us from the window.

All I could think about was how good my life was for me and my family. We played in the snow and made snowman; threw snowballs, and tried to bury each other in the snow. We played outside until our fingers and toes began to burn and itch or should I say, tingle.

Leroy started to cry shouting, "I'm cold. I want to go in the house". My mother heard Leroy from the window. I guess that's what you would call mother's ears. "Sherry", my mother yelled out the window, "bring your brothers and sisters in the house, it's time for y'all to come in".

This made Sherry mad because she wasn't ready to come in yet. As we entered the building and started to walk up the ramps that lead to the elevator, Sherry began to yell at Leroy, calling him cry baby, and punk. Sherry said that we made her sick and she couldn't wait until she didn't have to take us everywhere with her. We stood at the elevator and pushed the button that pointed up. Now that we were out of the cold, I noticed that I could no longer feel my feet. I started to shiver and my teeth started to chatter. The elevator door opens, Sherry yells, "hurry up y'all". She reaches over and presses the button for our floor. Leroy is still crying. "Shut up before I smack you boy!" threatens Sherry.

I mumbled to myself, "she thinks we are her kids". I wrap my arms around Leroy's neck slightly and whispered, "Shhhhhh!" I looked over at my lil' sister Rachel. She's standing there with a blank look on her face as if to say I can't help you twin we're all scared of her. The door opens, we make a left past the utility closet and the door to our apartment was already open.

When we entered the apartment things felt a little different. I'm too young to know what was going on, but it didn't feel like love was in the air. "Take off y'all coats and boots and put them on the newspaper that I put down on the floor in the closet" my mom said. All together we responded, "Yes" as if we were a choir. "Sit down and watch TV while the water boils for coco."

My stepfather keeps walking back and forth from the bedroom to the front door closet. The three bedroom apartment is not real big; you have the living room attached to a small kitchen. Five feet away to the left is the bathroom, to the right is my parent's bedroom, down the hall was the girl's bedroom and next to the girl's room was the boy's bedroom. I could see everything from where I was sitting. Everyone else was playing with their toys, but not me, I was too busy being nosey. My mom and stepfather were in the room having an argument on the low-low. I didn't want them to continue to argue so I said, "mom, the water is boiling". She pushed the door closed as she walked out the room while Bill was still talking, as if to say, shut the f _ _ k up! I asked my mom what was wrong, she answered, "nothing, just go play". We all drank our coco and went to our rooms to take a nap. For some reason I couldn't go to sleep. I sat up and looked out the window watching people come and go out of the other buildings. I counted cars as they passed by until I realized I stopped counting.

Sherry was the first to wake-up from the nap. She woke me up saying, "I think William left us." As I began to sit up, I asked her why did she say that? She said, because I saw him leaving with his clothes in boxes. I started to cry because he was a good dad to me. The rest of my siblings began to wake up one by one. Sherry told them exactly what she had just told me. Denay started to cry, but Leroy and Rachel didn't, neither did Chuck. I knew something was wrong, but my eyes wouldn't let me stay awake to find out what it was.

As we entered into the living room we noticed that someone had bust the windows out and my mom had a towel wrapped around her wrist and tears running down her face as she was tapping cardboard over the busted window. When she turned around to get the scissors, she noticed that we all were standing there. She tried not to let us see her crying, but it's too late, the house is a mess, it looks like they had a fight. We can't ask her what happened, so we all just stood there with tears in our eyes because we knew she was upset and hurting. So we started to help clean up the house in total silence.

She said it, "y'all dad is gone and he's not coming back, ok." But why is the question I asked in my head as tears continue to roll down my face. This is Christmas, what happen? We were just happy this morning. I guess she chased him away like she did our dad, now none of us had a father, I'm mad at her now. After cleaning up we ate dinner and sat down on the couch feeling like our world was just turned upside down

As each month passed by, the perfect family life began to make a drastic change. I regret the day William left our home. It felt like my mom stop caring for us each day that passed by. I noticed a change in the way my mom started to dress. She went from cooking three meals a day to cooking whenever she felt like it and from getting our hair done once a week to maybe once a month. Not only did we notice the difference our friends and neighbors did too. But, also they knew better than to ask her what happen to Bill or why we look like we do. I wanted to ask her myself, but she started beating us a little more then she did before. Now we were being beaten with extension cords and sometimes a broom. It all depended on how mad we made her. So I did what was best and just rolled with the punches. Sometimes my mom would get so caught up that she wouldn't even cook dinner for us or at the point where she would not come home at night. She would stay out three to four times a week. Whenever my mom didn't come home, she left my sister Sherry in charge. That meant she had to cook and clean, take care of our hair which made her mad, she was just a little girl like me, except she's a year older. I'm eight years old and she's nine. I must say Sherry keeps us in check.

Whenever there was nothing to eat in the house, Sherry would feed us a can of corn, beans, vegetables and sometimes cookies for dinner. We were no longer able to go outside and play because we spent most of our time left alone in the house without parental supervision. We had each other and that helped out a lot, but at times we missed our mom, especially Leroy and Rachel. We learned how to take care of each other when one of us felt down.

"Come on y'all get up and help me clean this apartment", said my mom. We asked each other, why is mommy so happy? She's lighting incense, making the house smell good, our hair is done, faces all shining with Vaseline. I think she's coming back to herself. "Yes", I thought to myself.

Where going out today! I managed to find something nice to put on. Everyone looks nice and we're sitting on the couch just waiting to hear the words "let's go". Still waiting.

I'm thinking.

She's putting on her lipstick and then there's a knock on the door. Mommy walks over to the door without even peeking through the peep hole and opens the door. "Hi baby", he says as he leans in to kiss her on the lips. "Is the kids here?" he asked while smacking her on the butt. "Yes, they're on the couch", she answers.

I'll never forget the way he looked. He was tall, dark skin with a low cut, slim build, but built like a boxer. His eyes more slanted more on the sneaky side, teeth the color of pearl. He looks nothing like my stepfather or my dad. Tall, brown skin with curly hair but that's not the point. The point is I don't like him!!!!!

"Hi little ones", is what he said with a deep voice. My name is Sam. We all looked at him with a look on our face like who's this cat mom. My brothers didn't even shake his hand, let alone say hi. Mommy gave us a look like don't make me hurt y'all. "Didn't Mr. Sam say hi?" mommy asked. "Hi", we responded. They sat at the table for a while to talk. In the meantime we sat on the couch like some nice little kids waiting at the bus stop, wondering when we were going to catch the bus or go out to play.

It never happened, she tricked us, all of that cleaning and dressing up was for H loser. We ate dinner, fried chicken, mash potatoes, string beans and cornbread followed by a tall glass of cherry Kool-Aid. Yummy that was good. "Okay y'all get washed and dressed for bed", mommy said. She never calls us by our name. We all gave her a kiss goodnight and started off to get ready for bed. "Did y'all forget something"? Mommy asked. "Good night Mr. Samson", we said. As we walked to the backroom, I whispered, "I don't like him do y'all"? Sherry responded "Hell No", she's the grown one and she curses all the time. We knew better than to tell on her. Before I fell asleep I prayed to the Lord God, please bring my stepfather back and get rid of this scary man and bless my brothers and sisters and grandmom, Amen.

This dude done moved in! Things are not as they seem they're starting to argue more and more. Mommy doesn't even care anymore. She's not acting the same. I think she's getting high or something. One day I walked by the room and saw them wrap this plastic string around their arms and smack theirs arms, then they stuck a needle in their arms. I stood on the side of the door wondering what they were doing. She didn't even see me; she was so busy doing whatever. I motioned for my big sister and we both watched them. They began to move in slow motion. Their voices started to change. The higher they got the more they fussed at each other. They called each other a mother f**ker and sometimes a b**ch!

I startled them by asking mommy if we could have something to eat. "Go and sit your f**king ass down", she said. That night we didn't have dinner. The next day was the same thing and so on and so on. We never saw mommy the same anymore. If she wasn't high, she was angry because they couldn't get high and they fought like cats and dogs, breaking and selling things. Instead of going food shopping, mommy started replacing food for drugs.

While this was happening, I realized that the devil had entered our home. He was tearing it apart, starting with the Queen. He entered her body in the form of drugs. He made her think that it was the only thing that loved and needed her. Sam became more important to her than her children. There was times when mommy would feed Sam and not us and he didn't even say a word. It was never enough for him no matter what she did, he was never happy.

All Sam wanted to do was have sex and fight. It got to the point that whenever they would fight we all went to our bedrooms until it was over. Mommy would sometimes come out with a black eye or busted lip. Sam would have scratches all over his face. We were afraid of him so we would sometimes stand there and cry. Embarrassed over the fact that we now knew what was going on, mommy started making excuses about why Sam was beating on her. "He's a nice man, he's just upset." She would say, "just go back in y'all room," motioning us to walk to the back of the room with a cold wet rag placed over her lips. I promised myself that I would never let a man beat on me like that or I'd just kill him in his sleep or stab the mess out of that nigga.

Now with mommy on this roller coaster relationship it's starting to interfere with our schooling. We started missing days back to back. The more she got high the more days we stayed out of class. At times mommy would get so high that my big sister would get us up and ready for school. Because she didn't know how to wash our clothes without a washing machine, she would take a wet rag and wipe off our jeans and look for a shirt that wasn't too dirty for us to put on and off to school we would go. When we did that it made my mom extra angry. That caused us all to get a whooping with extension cord. We all line up for the slaughter, shaking so bad, biting our nails, pleading with mommy not to hit us. We were just hungry and wanted some breakfast to eat.

We couldn't win for loosing; we all got a beating until her arms became tired. Whenever she was angry it didn't matter where the belt or extension cord fell on our body leaving cuts and bruises all over our body. I often thought how could a mother treat her beautiful babies so bad? What did we do to deserve this?

Now we're out of school for more days trying to wait until the scars and bruises heal. "I told y'all not to leave out of my house until I say so", mom would say trying to justify what she had done to us. "Y'all go to bed and there's no dinner tonight," mommy said. It didn't even hurt us no more because we were use to it by now. My big sister always had something put up for us to eat on days like these. We ate cookies and drank juice in the room and said our prayers. We talked about how we were beginning to hate our mother and we no longer wanted to be with her. My sister checked our sores and helped us all put on our pajamas and night gowns, then we all said goodnight. Sherry was so hurt and yet so strong that she never really showed her emotions, even when we got a whooping. I loved her because she was our protector, whom I'm very pleased with.

Finally, we can go to school, as we enter the school gates, my siblings and I immediately separate to find our own friends. I love to play in the school yard until the bell rings. I walked across the field and asked the girls could I play rope with them. "Yeah you can play, but you have ends," Brenda replied. I reached the rope and wrapped the ends around my hands and began to turn. It felt like hours, singing to the rhythm of the beat of the rope hitting the ground.

"All in together, this is the kind of weather, January, February, March, etc......" It's finally my turn, I yelled out "first", because I know that I was going to set the bars up as high as I could. I stood on the right side of one of the girls turning the rope. Motioning up and down, slightly lifting my feet off the ground to the rhythm of the beat of the rope. When the time was right, I leaped in the rope and ran like I was running for my life. Concentrating on not letting that rope hit me and making sure I did every order that was called out.

Whenever I jump rope it feels like I'm free from all the worries and cares. It feels like I'm flying. As I look at the faces of the people standing around I notice that they were getting angry, so I decided to stop. I was far enough that I felt safe. Just as the second girl began to enter the rope, the school bell rang. They were so mad at me saying "she took a long time, now I didn't get my turn." One of the other girls responded. "We'll finish at lunch time recess, in the same order."

Brenda and I walked to our line and stood behind next to each other to continue talking until our teacher Ms. Johnson walked up. "Good morning boys and girls, please quiet down. Get in two lines and let's go", said Ms. Johnson. Ms. Johnson told the first young man to grab the door so that we can enter the building and for the last young man to close the door. In class Ms. Johnson began to take roll. "When I call, you respond so that I know you're present." When she got to my name, she said welcome back Ms. Lewis. I was a little upset with her for making a fool out of me, "I thought." After the class settled down Ms. Johnson called me to her desk. "Why haven't you been to school young lady?" she asked. "Your grades are slipping", she responded. "What happened to your face?" I placed my head down looking at the floor and answered. "I fell off the bed," I told her. "That's what you told me last time, and the time before that. Go take your seat and start on today's assignment." Not knowing that Ms. Johnson had heard enough excuses and already reported my mom to the office to be checked by D.H.S.

During lunch time, I was called down to the nurse office and questioned again. The nurse also checked my body for bruises. She had a sheet of paper in her hand that looked like a picture of a body on it. The nurse began marking the sheet of paper putting an X on every part of the body she found a scar to match the paper. When we were done the nurse sent me to lunch. I didn't know that she called my brothers and sisters and did the exact same thing to them.

The day went by so fast all I remember was hearing the bell ring at the end of the day. "Don't forget to do your homework and be prepared for tomorrows test," Ms. Johnson reminded us. I grabbed my things, placed them in my book bag and stood in line. The teacher led the class out to the school yard where we all were dismissed.

I met up with my siblings making sure everyone was together; we began to walk home and talk about what happened to us at school. We didn't know we all had a visit with the nurse. Before we went into the building Sherry stopped at the Blue Truck to get some candy for us to share. We went into the building and decided to take the stairs because the elevator was taking too long. The door to our apartment was never locked, so we all walked in without knocking on the door. We already knew what we had to do so we immediately got started. Once we got home, play time was over and slavery began.

The phone is ringing off the hook today stated my mom. She walked over to the kitchen wall and grabbed the phone with aggression in her voice as she answers the phone. "Hello", she said standing with one hand on her hip and her eyebrows pointed towards the ceiling. "Yes, this is she. What? That's a lie! Listen,

I don't give a damn what nobody say, y'all don't tell me how to raise my kids. I had them, now you can tell whoever told you this bullshit that!" And she hung up the phone. I don't know what the person was saying on the phone, but it sure made mommy mad.

"I don't know what y'all little mother f**kers told them people at school, but the next time y'all tell anybody what goes on inside of my house, y'all are going to regret the day y'all was born", she proclaimed.

"Now these niggas want to be walking through my house, asking me all these questions and shit. Get the hell up and help me clean this damn place", she yelled. "Sam you got to pack your stuff and leave for a while because D. H. S. is on their way, she said. It didn't take him long to do that because he came with nothing but a few things and that's what he left with. I hope he's gone forever, I thought with a smirk on my face.

After Mr. Sam left and about an hour later there was a knock on the door. It sounded like the knock of a cop. I know the knock by heart now from living in the PJ's. You could barely hear the voice of the DHS worker as she shouted her name over the sound of the kids running up and down the hall. My mom looked out the peephole and mumbled "damn", followed by a stomp of her feet. Before she opened the door, mommy motioned with a wave of her hand for us to sit down somewhere. She opened the door and told her to come on in. This time she put on her nice lady voice. Ms. Barnes a very tall brown skin lady with a big Afro, thick hips walked in with a slight limp. "Hi little people", she said as she sat at the table to talk to mommy while looking around the room. My siblings and I sat there and watched television without saying a word like little manikins.

I heard the DHS worker say with a nice soft voice, "Ms. Lewis, I need to check the kid's room, the bathroom for running water hot and cold and also your refrigerator, okay?" Mommy said follow me this way, pretending to be a nice woman. After they finished the walk through of the rooms, they went straight to the fridge. There wasn't much in it, so Ms. Barnes scolded my mother with sternness in her voice, "the next time I visit your home you should have more food in the fridge." Mommy tries to talk over Ms. Barnes and says, "you know these kids eat a lot, breakfast, lunch and dinner, food goes fast around here." "Alright, but right now it's not enough food in here for your children, so do me and yourself a favor and go food shopping." The visit was finally over and she passed the test. Like the bible says what's done in the dark will come to the light!

Mommy done punched her hands through the window; it's blood all over the place. We didn't know what happened; my siblings and I were skating in the hallway with on skate a piece. We didn't have skates of our own so our friends shared theirs with us. "Oh shit", Sherry screamed, "they are fighting again and mommy is bleeding all over the place. The door flew open and instantly we started crying when we saw my mom fighting her boyfriend. There was nothing we could do but cry. My neighbors pulled us in their house and call the police. When the police came Mr. Sam was still in the house, so they walked straight in with their flashlights up and their guns drawn. "Get your hands up in the air now", yelled the police. They grabbed Mr. Sam and placed the handcuffs on him while asking "what's going on". Mommy yelling, "this mother f**ker keep putting his hands on me and I'm tired of him." The police officer then asked "did he do this to you?" "Yes he did", mommy replied. The officer then asked, "did you want to press charges on him?" My mom said, "you damn right I do. Get this b**ch out of here." "Ma'am you need to wrap your arm and we'll radio for the ambulance to take you to the hospital."

"I can't go any damn where, who's going to take care of my

kids? The officer then said, "you have children around watching you get abused. What are you thinking?"

"I don't know I was busy getting my ass kicked."

And that's when she yelled out our names from the oldest to the youngest and that's the same way we entered the apartment. With tears running down our face and shaking like a leaf. "

It's okay children, mommy will be okay" Then the officer turned to my mother and said, "ma'am if we come back to your home again we're taking the kids with us."

"What the hell does this have to do with them?" Mommy asked. "I didn't even call y

all mother fuckers anyways." They walked Mr. Sam out the door in handcuffs.

"Cindy, if you want to go to the hospital I'll watch the kids for you", replied our neighbor Ms. Bird. With tears in her eyes mommy responded, "Please, I'd be right back".

At that moment I didn't know if she was crying from being hurt or because her man had been arrested. The ambulance came and mommy shut the door to our apartment. That night we spent the night with Ms. Bird.

For some strange reason, mommy seemed very cheerful today. I noticed that she had a brand new ring on her finger. I don't know where she got it from, but it was very nice. Since Sam was gone things were starting to look up. It's not perfect, but it's getting better or at least I think so. Mommy is starting to pick herself up from our hell hole she'd been in.

"We're going to see grandmom today," said mommy."

Filled with excitement we all got dressed very quickly and left the house. It's a beautiful day and everyone is out sitting on the benches in front of the buildings.

My friends are out playing rope, the fly guys are at the basketball court running ball, while on lookers stood off to the side waiting for a chance to play in the next game. I'm so happy that Chuck could see it! When we reach grandmom's house we're greeted with the biggest hug ever. My oldest sister Tina lives with grandmom. She lives like a queen. She's never happy to see us, but ooh well. My aunt Tammy and her children live there along with my uncle Tommy. I love spending time with granny, so when everyone else went out to play I stayed behind to have a talk with my grandmom. As grandmom and I were talking, there was a knock on the door and my uncle went to answer it. Cindy yells, "Tommy, there is a gentle man at eh door for you!"

Uncle Tommy introduces himself to the visitor.

"Hi, I'm Tommy, Cindy's brother and you are?"

Sam is what I heard the voice say. She's in the living room replied uncle as he walked him in the area where we all sat. I couldn't believe my eyes. The Devil was back pretending to be such a nice man. Hello Ms. Lewis, I'm Sam, please to meet you is what he said as he shook grandmom's hand.

"Hey Nicole", says Sam.

I stood in disbelief, wiping my eyes to make sure that I wasn't seeing a ghost.

"Mommy, this is my husband Sam."

Oohh my god it's a big one was the look everyone had on their faces. When did this happen and how come we never met him before now was the questions flying around at once. It's a long story Cindy said.

"Well I guess congratulations are due, grandmom said with a slight grin on her face.

"I'm always last to know everything." My grandmom and I always had a special connection and right off the back she knew that I wasn't happy and that something was wrong. My uncle is not feeling him either. He's a Marine and I bet if he knew what this man was beating on his sister like a human piñata there would be a problem.

"Trina, come here" is what grandmom said. Trina is my nickname that grandmom called me. As we dried the dishes in the kitchen she asked, "What's the matter with you?" Just as I was about to tell her, I noticed that my mom was looking at me from across the room. One of her brows was raised and it looked like she said, say something and I'll break your neck! So I didn't.

"Umm grandmom, I'm ready to go outside and play before it gets too dark," I said. I could wait to tell Sherry what mommy did. As soon as I saw her I spilled all the beans and boy was she mad.

"I hate that black ugly nigga. He better not say anything to me ''cause I'm not scared of him amymore," she said.

Here they come now all happy looking like two love birds.

"I'll see y'all later" is what mommy said as they stepped down the front steps. We were all gathered up and said our goodbyes and off we went down the block pretending to be one happy family.

Chapter 2

MOMMY SAID WE'RE MOVING

*I*t's two years later, my how time flies. Mommy said we're moving. Our boxes are pack and each box was labeled so that we knew whose belongings they were. We're moving on up like George and Louise except, we're moving from the high rises into the row homes. Yes!!!!

No more climbing those stairs, smelling piss in the elevator, no more walking through the halls in the dark. I sang out loud as I placed the tape across my boxes. Wait a minute. I stopped to think for a moment, with one finger on my bottom lip. This means we're moving across the street from grandmom. I don't even care that the raggedy old devil is coming with us.

The boys are in their room jumping in and out of their boxes. They were making all kinds of noises.

"Stop all that playing and hurry up before the truck comes. If y'all are not done it's going to be hell to pay!" yelled mommy. Mommy has been real happy now days even with them still arguing. He hasn't put his hands on her since he met her brother. "Mommy, we're done", said Sherry.

"Ok say goodbye to the neighbors and your friends, maybe you'll see them outside sometimes."

"The truck is here! Grab the boxes that go upstairs first, put them in the back. Then put the beds, living room set and refrigerator and let's move out!"

We made sure the house was swept, mopped and in top condition before turning out the lights to say our last goodbyes.

The four oldest children walked to the new home because there wasn't enough room in the truck. Mom and her husband made it to the new home before us so they started unpacking the truck. The neighbors were welcoming us into the neighborhood. I can tell off the back that some of the neighbors are nosey. We moved into the house at the end of the block. It has a big back yard fenced in. The kitchen was separated from the dining room and the living room. There were four bedrooms and one bathroom. We loved it!. Anna B. Pratt Arnold is going to be our new school. I can't wait to meet new friends.

On this particular day for some strange reason, I woke up extra early. I just happened to look out my bedroom window admiring the fact that we are now in one of the row homes that I often wished I could live in. As I'm looking out the window I noticed my stepfather William leaving out of this women's house right across the street from us. She hands him a brown paper bag and leans in to give him a kiss on the lips and a big hug goodbye.

I couldn't believe my eyes. I thought that I would never see him again. My heart leaped with joy. Just to see his face again brought joy to my little heart. At the same time I began to get angry thinking how could he just forget about his family like that and start all over like we never existed. After watching him leave out of my eye sight I slammed the window shut so hard that I woke up my sister Quay and I told her what I just saw. When mommy finds out, boy is it going to be trouble we said as we went downstairs to open the front door to get a better look. We went to the front door of the ladies house to get her address . We need to find out her name and if she has any kids. I'm determined at this point to end that relationship so that my stepfather will come back home where he belongs. My sister and I shook hands and agreed to work together to make it happen.

As I was closing the door I noticed this girl looking at us

across the walkway from my house. I licked my tongue and shut the door in her face, while calling her nosey. I told my sister not to tell mommy what we saw today. She listens to me. I had faith in her that my secret was safe. We're too young to cook so we made us a bowl of cereal and milk. When we were done we sat on the couch until everyone in the house woke up.

Mom woke up and there was not much for us to do since everything is finally unpacked and in its proper place. We asked mommy could we go out to play after we get dressed. She responded yes but not until everyone is dressed. We quickly did what she asked and off we went to accomplish our mission. We went across the street on Edgley side where we knew some of the kids already. We started playing rope and that 'cause more girls to come out and play. Then I notice a little girl coming out of the house I saw my stepfather come out of earlier, she was younger than my sisters and I so I couldn't be mean to her. She was a pretty little girl with China

doll eyes, long hair and light brown skin complexion. The strange thing was that we got along very well. We played together all that day. I didn't tell Rachel, Leroy or Denay that their dad had moved in with this woman and her family across the street from us. I figured they would find out in enough time. It was a little after six o'clock when my stepdad came home. We all were playing on his block. When he walked up the block we all ran up to him, including the little girl, with opened arms grabbing whatever empty space on his body that we could wrap our arms around. He gave us love in return letting us know that he missed us too. We followed him home telling him that we live across the street pointing to our house. His eyes grew bigger. We could tell he was a little upset when we told him where we lived. He introduced us to his new lady named.... are you ready for this one...Cindy! It was funny that she already knew about us, we just didn't know about her yet. China was happy; she called us her brothers and sisters. Denay was not happy and everyone knew it. She had her arms crossed and her lip dropped towards the floor. Denay was his first born and she looked just like him, but has the attitude of my mother. Before it got too dark outside, Bill gave us all some money and sent us home. As we crossed the street I felt so safe just knowing that our dad lived so close to us. No one said a word about what happened today as we sat at the table to have dinner.

I'll be right back, said mommy as she quickly slipped on her sweat shirt and brushed her hair to the back wrapping it tightly with a rubber band. Before leaving out the front door, mommy grabbed a scoop of petroleum jell, rubbed her hands together and quickly wiped her face with it. She was moving so fast that the front door never shut completely. I walked behind her and stood in the door trying not to be seen wanting to know exactly where she was headed. For a moment I thought she was going to Ms. Cindy house, but she knocked on the door right next door to her house. That was close, I thought to myself. I saw my mom banging on this lady's door like she was the cops. When the woman finally answered, I couldn't hear what was being said. All I saw was mommy hand all up in the lady face tapping her forehead with her pointer finger. Then all of a sudden I saw mommy punch her on the side of her face. My eyes grew so big; I couldn't believe what was happening. I started screaming out for my sister Sherry, telling By the time Sherry made it to the front door they were fighting on the lawn in front of the lady house. Mommy had her by her hair dragging her while the lady continued to kick trying to land a few of them. Everyone started coming outside to get a better view. All of a sudden, who walks out the lady's house, Mr. Sam! He was just standing there watching them fight. My mom was punching the lady all in the face (she's a beast). I guess he had seen enough so he decided to break the fight up, pulling my mom by the waist saying Cindy let her go baby it's over. Oh why did he do that? That's when she turned and proceeded to whoop on his ass. Mom started yelling, "you no good nigga, I can't believe you, kiss my ass, I'm through with you! I hate your black ass!" And she just kept slapping the hell out of him.

"This is where you been at? Answer me!" she said while pushing him at the same time.

"Listen Cindy, enough is enough," he responded, while giving her a push that landed her on the ground. Now we're crying and yelling at her, "no mommy no!", while she tries to get up he starts slapping her, calling her a stupid bitch. That's when the men from around the neighborhood stepped in and started snatching Mr. Sam by his shirt and gripping him up. My stepfather came out his house with his new lady watching in disbelief. When mommy noticed them she started cursing him out. Yelling, "what the hell you looking at? Is this where you live? Come get your fucking kids since you want to play daddy!"

I felt so bad for mommy; she was hit with a double whammy. As mommy made her way back across the street the police pulled up. The neighbors pointed right across the street toward our house. I'm sure that the lady called when she finally got off the ground and made her way to her house.

"Ma'am, wait one minute I need to talk to you," said one of the officers. Mommy kept walking acting like the cop wasn't talking to her. "Get in the house and stop crying I'm ok," my mom said. The cops made their way to our house to question mommy. That's when I found out what happened. Sam was cheating on mommy with the woman across the street and she knew that they were married. Mommy told the police how her husband had bust her lips as she wiped her mouth with her shirt. "Where is he, asked the police?" Mom pointed across the street describing what he was wearing. The partner of the officer came over to make sure everything was ok. "Ms. Lewis I know that it's not you again, stated the officer. Didn't I tell you that the next time I came out I was taking your kids?" They called for backup as they proceeded to lock Mr. Sam up, he ran. Some of the cops chase him on foot while the others drove in the cars.

Later that day DHS came out and was about to take us with them. Before we grabbed our jackets the DHS worker asked mommy did she have a relative she could call to let us come stay with them for a while or else we were going with her. Mommy gave them my grandma's phone number. Grandmom, Uncle Tommy and Aunt Tammy walked around the corner to come and get us. Uncle Tommy was so upset after he heard what happened from the cops. Please sign this sheet Ms. Lewis, the DHS worker said before she handed us over to grandmom while the police placed mommy under arrest. Before putting the cuffs on mommy the police allowed her to change her shirt and lock the doors. As we made our way through the crowd, I looked back and saw the cops open the door to the backseat of the car giving mommy's head a slight push forward so that she could get in. Uncle Tommy turned my head around and said, "Trina, you don't need to see that."

That night Sam came back for revenge, he must have heard through the grape vine that mommy was looked up. He tried to come in our house and hide out for a while not knowing that my mom had been released that night. He came in through our back door and made his way up the stairs. I guess to rest his worried mind. That's when he noticed my mom sleeping in her bed. That very night he raped my mom and beat her up at the same time. When he was done with her he threw her outside in the snow naked for everyone to see. He called her all kinds of names ahs he ran back in the house grabbing her clothes, setting fire in all parts of our home. It didn't take much time before the whole house went up in smoke. The next-door neighbor came outside after hearing moaning sounds in the back of her house. She grabbed my mommy and placed a sheet around her and called the police.

Mr. Sam didn't leave out the same way he came in. This time he left out from the front door. Just as he was leaving out, he walked right into Uncle Tommy. They exchanged a couple of words and the fight was on. Uncle Tommy said, "you like hitting my sister, hit me nigga!" Uncle Tommy continued to punch Sam in his face. This dude supposed to be a boxer, but it seems like he lost this round.

Mr. Sam yelled out, "I didn't rape her; she wanted it so I gave it to her. What y'all going to do about that? Mr. Sam, trying to speak with blood leaking out of his mouth. We couldn't believe our eyes; our home was burning right in front of our eyes. Uncle wouldn't let Sam go this time. He kept him there until the cops came. "Officer, officer, yelled the neighbors, that man over there in the white shirt and brown cut off pants and black boots is the one who set the fire and beat that woman up." The officer said, "say no more we already had a warrant for his arrest." They quickly grabbed him and placed the cuffs on him whispering in his ear, "they won't be seeing you for a long while."

Mommy yelled out, that mother fucker raped me and I want to press charges. The officer said, "you need to go down to the district and place a complaint and restraining order for your protection. You may not be so lucky the next time."

"Who said I'm lucky. Now my children and I don't have a place to stay." Mommy went with the police to the hospital to be checked out. Then we headed back to grandma's house after everything was over with.

"Grandmom, now what are we going to do, I asked."

You're going to be fine, don't you worry ok. That's my job.

Your mommy needs a lot of help. Let's go home and put your brothers and sisters to bed and get ready for school tomorrow."

"Yes ma'am."

When Uncle Tommy came home his lip had a little cut on it but besides that he was my hero. I knew that he could do it. He beat that man like he stole something. At that moment I thought life was beautiful, as long as I had my granny. I knew that we would be ok.

Chapter 3

LIVING WITH GRANNY

*I*t's like clockwork every Saturday grandmom washes our hair and gives us five huge plats until our hair dries. We didn't have a hair dryer so once it dried my Aunt Tammy would press it out with the straightening comb so that it would look nice for Sunday morning service. Grandmom didn't cook dinner on Saturdays she usually made hotdogs and beans or lunchmeat and cheese sandwiches. We loved it. We didn't have the finest of things, but it sure felt better than the raggedy things we once wore. We sometimes went to the five and dime store to purchase clothes on Saturday. We all had our own clothes and we felt very pretty, for the boys I'll say handsome. I watched the faces of my love ones change from a worried look to the look of happiness. I myself began to feel care free. Every time I went outside to play I no longer had to stay around my friends waiting for them to have dinner praying that I would be offered a plate. I went home at a reasonable time and made it home for dinner every night.

I haven't seen my mom in a while and deep down inside I wish her the very best, but I still don't want to see her.

We almost always ate dinner together and talked about how our day went. When dinner was done we all cleaned the house together and when we were finished grandmom would always play board games with us. She was teaching us how to make the best of every moment together.

I greeted each member at the entrance of our church, dressed in black and white. "Praise the Lord was how I was taught to greet each member and visitor. I felt good directing them to a seat. I'm getting older now and I'm really starting to understand more and more how good God has been to my family and me. I can see the happiness on grandma's face as she stands up to give her testimony. "I would like to give all praise and honor to God for my health and family. I thank you Lord for keeping me another day. Thank you Lord for my granddaughter, thank you for helping her to open her heart to allow you to lead and direct her path." When grandmom finished I gave her a slight smile letting her know that I knew she was proud of me. the pastor stood up and started praying while the pianist played a tune. The choir marched in and began to sing, time waited for no one. Before I knew it we were collecting the tithes and offerings. I was too young to count the money that was collected, but old enough to carry it to the back where the older ushers calculated the money. As I made my way back to my post, I began to thank God for where he brought me. Tears rolled down my face and joy filled my heart. I love being in the house of the Lord and I truly love my pastor at Salem Mission Baptist Church.

"Let the church say, Amen! Turn around and hug your neighbor," I heard the pastor saying. The crowd is slowly moving out of the church, but I can't leave until everyone is out, the fans are collected and put in its proper place, there are no tissues left behind on the benches and all the tissue boxes are in their proper place. I gave Mother Johnson a quick hug and kiss and made my way to Mother Jenkins car where grandmom and my siblings waited for me. There's no place like home I thought to myself. I can't wait to take off these clothes and rest my aching feet. "Thank you sister," Granny said as we got out of the car. I waited with Granny while my siblings ran to the house. We walked through the playground on the side of our house and talked about what we were going to cook for dinner.

The basketball court was filled with niggas talking crap. "Hi Ms. Lewis," the guys on the sideline yelled. "Hello young men" Granny replied with a wave of her hand. I don't worry too much about Granny because everyone knew her even the drug dealers have respect for her. Thank you Lord, I thought to myself as I shut the front door.

"Grandmom, I have a friend name Camill who lives across the street from the Shopping Bag Supermarket, can I please go over her house for a little while?" I asked.

"Exactly where does she live?" Granny asked.

"On Glenwood, around the bend." I said.

"I want you back before eight and not a minute later!"

I grabbed my rope and my jean jacket, gave granny one of the biggest kisses ever and I was out. It felt so good to get off of the block. I made my way pass the neighbors, waved, said my hellos and kept it moving. I ran into so many of my friends on the way. I stopped to talk for a while, a long while 'cause time went by fast. It's so much better on this side of the projects, I thought to myself as I continued on my way to my friend's house. I saw so many faces of guys I have never seen before. They didn't know my age and I didn't care to tell them. I noticed them staring at me like I was a piece of meat on a bone.

I finally arrived at my friends. I knocked on the door and her little sister answered.

"Who is it? She asked.

"Katrina," I answered.

"Who are you and whom do you want?" She asked as she rolled her eyes at me.

"My name is Katrina and I am here to see Ashley, is she here?"

"Yeah she here, wait here and I'll get her"

This little girl seemed too grown with her evil self. I don't think I'm going to like her much, I thought. While I stood there waiting, three guys went in the house talking trash to each other.

"Who you?" The little one asked with a squeaky voice.

"I'm Katrina and I'm waiting for Ashley."

"Oh, Ok what's up, my name is Jimmy this is my little brother scotty and my big brother Tikey he said.

As I was waving hello Ashley was coming down the steps.

"Hey girl you ready?"

"Yeah," I responded as we walked out the front door to play rope with her friends on the block. This block is popping. It's a lot of kids around here. We had so much fun together; I think that Ashley and I are going to be best friends "cause we clicked real good. We stepped for a while and as soon as we started a crowd formed around us. We all had the moves and stayed on bet together. When they called my name I shouted and started moving my body as if I was using a hula hoop, causing the boys eyes roam to places they should never be. The strange thing was I liked it and I felt like I had so much power. As I was stepping I saw this boy that I liked, his name is Man. He's fine. I think I'm going to come around her more often.

The sun started going down and I knew that I needed to be on my way home. I gave Ashley a hug and said my goodbyes then started on my way home. As I was walking down the hill I glanced over at a family chilling in their backyard together whishing that God would bless me with a loving family of my own. Just as quick as the thought came to my head I quickly dismissed it "cause I knew it would never come true. I had to hurry up, so I took the short cut through the playground and before I knew it I was walking up my block.

To my surprise granny was sitting outside on the steps with Aunt Tammy, and one of my cousins. I tried not to notice Granny looking down at her watch to see if I made it on time. I was so happy I did, just by the skin of my teeth. I kissed Granny on her cheek and said my hellos then made my way in the house. I feel tired so I'm going to get ready for bed. As I started to take my clothes off, I really took notice of my body for the first time. My boobs are getting big and my butt has a nice little hump to it. I'm really starting to feel myself right now and I don't think that I'm going back to church anymore ''cause I'm having more fun in the streets. Forget this Jesus stuff. It's too hard for me to be a good girl. I laid down to go to bed and I don't even think I said my prayers ''cause I fell asleep so fast.

DISAPPEARING ACT

I'm tired of being Cinderella. Let someone else do this crap. I have big sister who does nothing. I'm out. I quickly go dressed and left. This time I didn't even ask my Granny could I go, I just left. And to make things worse, it was Sunday morning. I would usually get myself ready for church. I decided to go out with my friends. I knew my Granny would be angry with me but at this time in my life I didn't care anymore.

We met up in the back field and practiced the steps we made up together, so that we would be ready for our challenge later on that day. Our moves were so tight. The beats we made were awesome. I can't believe that I have found a new family. We have so much in common; the same family issues and everything. We made a vow that we would never let anyone hurt us. If we had to fight for each other then so be it. I love these guys and I'm having fun, that's all that matters.

Ashley's big brother Tiky went to the Speak Easy to get us a couple Forty Beers. We paid him for going, and then we sat outside on the monkey bars and go wasted. We cracked jokes about each other and laughed so hard. I didn't even check in with my grandmom to let her know that I was ok. For some reason I didn't care.

Our crew is getting so big it's crazy. I can't remember who brought the weed. All I do remember is that I have bitten off more than I could chew. It feels like I'm on a roller coaster that's moving really fast. Some of us could handle it better than others. I was one of them that couldn't hang, but I played it off like I could. I didn't tell them that this was my first time. I stood there in silence praying to myself, God please make this spinning in my head stop. The only thing helped me was when this strange feeling shot from my stomach to my throat. I grabbed my mouth and ran off to the side and let it rip. It was like a volcano erupting as I poured my guts out on the grass.

They all laughed and called me a nut, but it was all in fun. We got ourselves together and rounded everyone up for the show down. In another hour it was on and poppin'. I placed a piece of gum in my mouth to make sure the breath was fresh and clean. It was so many of us, as soon as I opened my gum it was gone. If you didn't get one shame on you was my thought.

It's show time! Here come the girls that we're about to challenge. We tossed a quarter, my crew chose heads and they lost, so they had to go first. Everyone got in position and shouted out "Mississippi hit it!" I admit it they were ok, but we were great, high and all. Our first step was called "Look b**ch Don't Switch!" We performed steps that we made up ourselves and it always took our opponents by surprise ''cause we were original. As the crowd grew bigger the hyper things got. Sometimes we would get mad at the other group, but we tried not to let it get in the way of having fun.

We won!!! Yeah!!! It was over and now time for me to go home and face the music. Whatever happens it was worth it. Nothing could ever take away this feeling that I have right now. Finally being a part of something that has no rules, or grown-ups telling me what, when, and how to say what I'm feeling. I'm scared a little, but oh well. I slowly open the door.

I can't sleep. Some nights it feels as if someone is holding me down in my sleep. I tried to scream but no words are coming out. I feel my lips moving but I can't hear my voice. Let me go, get off of me, Grandmom help me, I'm shouting. My eyes are opened, I can see but I can't move. Suddenly all I could remember was what the pastor said in church, "whenever the devil attacks plead the blood of Jesus and shall bow to His name and flea." So I began to shout from the depths of m soul....the blood of Jesus. I started to feel freed and "Jesus" was all I heard myself say.

I quickly jumped up out of the bed and turned on the light. I looked to the left, then to the right. I'm scared. I snatched back the curtains that covered my closet. There was nothing there. Not really wanting to look I bent down and looked under my bed to make sure nothing was there. I want to get in the bed with my grandmom, but I'm a big girl now, so I took my dumb ass back to bed. But this time I slept with the light and television on. My attitude stinks and I don't care. I do whatever I have to do in the house and leave. My Granny doesn't even ask me to go to church anymore. I don't think I'm one of her favorites anymore. We don't talk like we use to.

These boys got me on some other stuff. They're coming at my neck. My stuff is hot and I think I'm ready for some. If I hadn't started kissing boys I don't think I would be having this feeling, that I'm feeling. Whenever I go out I have to look my best. My hair needs to be done and my lips need to shine. I love wearing tight jeans that make my butt look bigger than it really is. When

I hit the door it's all about me. I'm looking for love. A hug, a kiss, a touch, whatever it takes, I'll do it. I don't like this feeling that I'm feeling, not being wanted by my mom or dad. It's starting to make me hate the world and everything in it.

Chapter 4

LOOKING FOR LOVE
IN ALL THE WRONG PLACES

O h my God, is just what I said when I saw this guy named Freddy. Of course he's older than me, but that doesn't matter. I turned to my friend Ashley of whom I've known almost all of my life. Now if you are talking about a true friend, she is it! She has my back and I have hers. Ok, so the whole time we were talking I was staring at this fine young man playing ball. The way he runs up and down the court with those sexy bow legs were turning me on. I'm watching the way his bulge looked. Maybe it's just me, but it's something I have developed. I can tell exactly where the head of his penis was and from what I can see, he's been blessed. I like what I saw and wanted it bad. After looking down so long, I decided to glide my eyes up his body slowly just to see if he had the whole package. As I made my way to his chest, it was medium build. Then his neck and finally to his face. He's a caramel brown complexion; he has beautiful dimples and a nice bone structure. Our eyes met and he gave me a smile and I smiled back. I guess I was caught.

"Hello! Hello! Katrina, I'm talking to you! Oh my God girl what are you thinking about? You didn't hear anything I just said?"

"I'm Ashley I'm looking at him."

"Who?"

"The guy right there?" I'm frustrated now "cause she's acting dumb." Its bad enough he caught me looking. Ashley responded, "I know you're not talking about Freddy the freak?"

"Yes! I am. I want him and I'm going to get him"

"Girl you ready?" asked Ashley.

"What am I ready for?" I ask.

"To leave I have to go home and do something for my mom. All right, I said let's go and we left. In the back of my mind I wanted to get his digits, but decided to wait until I got another chance to see him.

While walking to Ashley's house I asked her why she called him a freak. She said, "Because all he does is mess with young girls." I didn't care "cause I just wanted to know what he felt like inside of me. So I decided to change the subject.

"Anyway b**ch, we still going to the "Dollar Holla" tonight?"

"Yeah, that's why I'm going home to do whatever my mom wants and to get some money, so I could get in the party."

"If she doesn't give you the money I got you."

"Cool," she said.

It's never a dull moment in her house. She has two sisters and three brothers. Everyone has their own set of friends that was at the house when we got there. We had a blast. It was like the party already started. I stayed down stairs while Ashley went upstairs with her mom. I thought Ashley mom was so cool. She let us do whatever we wanted to do, if she was in a good mood. It was a Friday night and everybody was excited about the party. We decided to go half on the forties and the weed. Ashley's brother Tiky was old enough to get the drinks and weed. We always had to give him a little extra to go for us, plus allowing him to get high with us. We all put our money in and got the party started.

It's about time to roll out. "If y'all are ready we can all leave together," I said.

"Hold up," said Ashley's big sister.

"Before y'all leave clean up y'all mess before mommy get up and cuss me out over the mess y'all dumb ass left."

"That b**ch gets on my nerves. She thinks she's somebody's mom." Her little sister would say.

All of them that didn't get to high, got up and cleaned and then we left.

This party is out of control. It's crowded as hell. All the niggas are in the house. We made our way to the back of the house, that's where we like to hang out, that way we can see everything that was going on. I'm leaning on the wall ''cause I'm high as hell and it's hot. Ashley is dancing. Everyone else scattered, but I can still see everyone.

I started to make my way to the front door when my song comes on, or should I say our song. It's like a bell went off in our head. Everyone in our dance group made way to the middle of the floor to dance. It was time to show the Hood our dance step we made up off of the Show by Doug E. Fresh. It was Ashley, Leslie, Mia, Rhonda, Keonna, Valeria, Abena, Ebony and I. We backed people up so fast and blew the roof off the mother sucker. I was looking around at every face in the room. I could see their expressions in their eyes. the girls were mad and the boys were happy. The song ended and we exited the dance floor just as fast as we entered it.

"Damn Ashley, I'm going out for some air," I said.

"Ok I'll be here."

I go outside and a couple of girls from around the way give a compliment on how good we were.

"Thanks," I say. My heart is still racing. Breathing slow seems to calm the rhythm of my heart down. I see Freddy walking up with a couple of his friends. "What's up?" He says with a nod of his head.

"Hi", is all I could get out of my mouth. Suddenly those desires start to surface. I watch him enter the house and thought to myself, I got to have him.

I waited a while and then went back in the party. Damn time went by so fast. It was a quarter to one. That meant I only had an hour to dance and at least try to make my move. Yes! I said move! The party is beginning to empty out. Now you can see everybody better. Ashley was slow dancing with one of Freddy's friends. That left me standing by myself. Out of nowhere he tapped me on my shoulder and asked if I'd like to dance. Sure, I thought you'd never ask; is what I was thinking. Not even waiting for an answer, he grabbed my hand and took me to the wall. I leaned back and opened my legs as if I was saying come on in. *I Call Your Name* by DE barge was playing. Our eyes locked, he laid his chest on mine and I wrapped my arms around his waist with his arms around my neck, we slowly began to move in a circular motion. His skin is ever so soft. He smells OOOOHHHH so good. He's whispering in and licking my ears slowly. It feels so good. By now his nature is rising and that's when I knew he was huge. My panties are so wet by now and my mind is going a mile a minute. He's touching me in places he shouldn't but I like it and I want more. I slid my hand down the side of his leg just so I could feel it. He liked it and asked me where I was going after the party.

"Home," I responded.

While I was talking he swept his lips passed mine and we began to tongue lock. I was high and I didn't care who saw what. I was concentrating on what I wanted and that I wanted him. The music stopped, but I wanted to keep dancing the night away. The light came on, it was two o'clock in the morning and someone shouted, "you don't have to go home, but you got to get the hell out of here!" Freddy and I exchanged numbers and left the party.

"Girl, I saw you and Freddy over there acting like y'all are together or something."

"I saw you girl. I had a good time tonight."

We gave each other a high five and separated on Twenty-Third and Edgley Street.

While walking in complete silence, all I could do was think about him. By the time I made it in the house he was calling. I ran to get the phone before it woke grandmom up. I grabbed the phone on the second ring. When I answered Freddy said that he was checking to see if I gave him the right number.

"Well you see I did and you're going to get me in trouble."

"Can you come back out?" He asked.

"No, I just came in," I said.

"Can you sneak out? I'm trying to see you"

"I want to see you too. Hold on and let me call my cousin to see if she'll come out with me. Who's hanging with you?" I asked.

"My boy," he says.

"We'll bring him with you for my cousin that way she won't feel left out"

"Ok," Freddy says, "call me back when you're done talking to her."

"Will do," I say as we hang up.

My cousin Nikki is always down for whatever, so I took a chance on calling her. She always answers on the second ring.

"Who is it," she whispers.

"It's me, Trina." I say.

"Girl what do you want? She asked.

"Girl I met this guy and he has a friend and they're both fine!" I explained to her.

"Girl you know I can't come back out," she says.

"We're going to sneak out," I said.

"Sneak out!"

"Yeah! Girl hold on, let me hang up on the other line."

"Nikki, are you down or what I asked?"

"Let me see if my mom is still sleep."

Full of excitement and anticipation, I couldn't wait to hear her say, yes!

"Come on, come on, come on, I kept saying, waiting for her to get back on phone. Finally she picks the phone up and says, "Ok, He better not be ugly."

"He's not. Meet me at the field I say as we hang up the phone.

I couldn't hang up any faster. I dialed Freddy's number so fast that I dialed the wrong number. Damn! What's taking him so long to answer? He picked up and I asked him what took him so long to answer. The voice on the other end says, "first of all who dis?" That's when I realized that I must have dialed the wrong number. This time I took my time making sure I dialed the correct number. He answered on the first ring in a low soft sexy voice.

"Hello, is it on?" He asked.

"Yes," I said, trying to sound sexy.

"Where you want to meet up at?" I ask.

"In front of building 09 and don't take all night. I'll be there so make sure your friend comes ''cause my cousin is coming."

I grabbed my keys and tip toed to the front door. I held both hands on the door knob and turned it real slow trying not to make a sound. I cracked open the door halfway and slid out. I shut the door and began walking. I am a crazy b**ch, ''cause if my Uncle would have caught me, it would have been my ass. I laughed to myself and kept it moving. I met up with Nikki in no time. As soon as she sees me she says, "Girl we are always doing something crazy." I looked her over quickly as we walked. Nikki has an ass that looked like she just picked up two basketballs and placed them in the back of her jeans as an add on. She has a light brown complexion. She is short and bow legged. She always wore a short hair style. Nikki wore pants so tight that you could see her vagina print. She had a walk that made grown men cry, so I knew his friend would be happy, but will she be happy I thought to myself.

We both smelled and looked good. We talked the whole time on our way there. "I can see him from here," I say. Trying to stay calm 'cause my insides was shouting he came. Finally we're face to face. Freddy introduces his friend Tommy to Nikki. I could see he liked what he saw and so did Nikki. The feeling was definitely mutual.

Damn! Tommy looks even better but I like what I see in Freddy too. We began to walk up the ramp to get inside the building. We took the elevator to the tenth floor. There was nothing but silence the whole ride up. He grabbed my hand and we walked to the apartment 1004. When we walked in I noticed that there was not an adult in sight. Nikki came in right behind us. We all sat down for a minute. Then Freddy grabbed my hand and we walked to the back room. Oh my god it's about to happen and I'm scared to death because truth be told I am still a virgin.

It's dark with a little touch of light. Two beds were in the room and a tall dresser. On top of the dresser was a 13" television. That's all I could see, as he lead me to one of the beds.

"Watch yourself," he said as he sat on the bed. He places his hands in my hair ever so gently and began to massage my head with his fingertips. "MMMMMM" is all I could say, but in the back of my mind I'm thinking he's a pro at this. He didn't spend any time at all talking. This was the first time my nipples were touched by a man and it felt so damn good. My body began to relax as he rotated his tongue up and down the twins, not allowing one to be jealous of the other. My legs began to shake. "Don't be scared," he says in a soft voice. I started to say but I'm a virgin, but he told me to "Shhh," before I could finish my sentence. He makes his way to my navel. That made me wiggle, sending a sensation through my body that made me hungry for what it felt like in the middle of my love nest.

Me being nosey I wanted to feel it first, so I reached down with one hand and began to give it a jerk. I noticed that the more I jerked it, the longer it got, so I kept jerking and massaging it until my hand became sticky and wet. It must of felt good "cause he started to moan and hum things that I'll never forget like, " umm girl what the f*ck are you doing, you are about to make me nut and I haven't even been in you yet."

"Don't do that," I managed to say as I licked my lips, waiting to feel his long thing. Will it hurt or will it feel good is what my mind began to say. Stay cool, just relax, I told my body and it soon did obey.

He opened my legs and lifted them to his waist side and gave me a look as to say open them up isn't this what you came for. I then gave him a look please don't hurt me. He grabbed his manhood with one hand and placed his rubber on with the other. He played with my clit just to keep the juices flowing. I'm soaking wet, but still flinching at his every move. He then grabbed the head of his penis and placed it gently in the center of my thighs. With his pointer finger and middle finger he began to open the lips of my vagina wide. His head was so big I was nearly balling in tears. It hurts as he forces his way inside.

"Wait! wait! Is this shit supposed to hurt?" I asked.

"Do it?" He said, not missing a beat.

I'm making all kinds of noises "cause this doesn't feel good, not at all. I'm scratching his back and biting my lip trying to pretend like I can handle it, but the harder he stroke and the deeper he went, it felt like my asshole split.

"OOOHHHH baby this shit is good. Stop running and be a big girl."

He lost himself in his own moans and groans which seemed to get louder the faster he went and before I knew it his body started jerking and then it just went limp. "Damn girl!" He says as he rolled over to get off of me as he went to wash his manhood. I sat in complete silence not knowing what to say. I then got up to retrieve my things and went in the bathroom right behind him to wash myself clean. But before I walked into the bathroom I took a peak at the clock. It was 3:35 am; oh I know I'm really in for it. I made my way to the bathroom hoping to see Nikki. She was nowhere in sight. She must be getting her freak on too. Freddy passed me a clean rag as he walked out and I walked in. The soaps over there and I put one more rag out for your friend. Standing at the sink I started to feel like he raped me. Blood was on the rag as I washed myself totally clean. He busted my cherry and now I crossed over from a child to a sexually active teen. I got myself together and came out of the bathroom. One thing I noticed about myself was that I wasn't walking the same as I did when I first met him... I was in so much pain and all I could think about was going home and taking a bath so that I could try to close my vagina up. As I'm coming out the bathroom, Nikki was waiting outside of the door. She asked me was I ready and we walked right out the door. I don't think we even said goodbye. While waiting for the elevator we began to snap back to reality. We are going to be in a whole lot of trouble when we get home.

I asked Nikki did she give him some sex and she said, "yeah." Then she asked me the same question and I told her I did. We then decided next time we were going to stay in the same room. I just wanted her to be quiet. It wasn't working. I am still trying to figure out if I just got raped or was my first time a total disaster.

Her lips kept moving, but I heard no sound. It was like I pushed a pause button and put that b**ch in freeze mode. Sike! Let me stop. Deep down I was scared because if my uncle is up I am in trouble. So how am I going to get back in and act like I'm sleep? When I finally snapped back to reality this girl was still talking about how she had such a good time and wanted to go back. We're finally back to our starting point.

"All right Trina, Nikki say, I'll see you tomorrow.

"Bye freak," I say.

"Takes one to know one," she says.

As I'm walking up the walkway towards the front door my heart starts skipping a beat. My hands are sweating and my mind is racing. I began to walk up the steps and took a deep breath. Well here goes nothing. I rubbed my hands on the side of my jeans. I took one hand and placed it over the knob, with the other hand I unlocked the top lock, gently twisting the lock as quiet as possible. While twisting the knob I gave the door a slight push. The door opened without making a sound, but to my surprise the chain was placed on the door from the inside.

"Shit! Shit! Shit! I said jumping around. I sat my dumb ass down on the steps and began to cry. If I knocked on this door my ass is grass. I stopped crying and picked up this stick from off the ground and began to stick it between the cracked door.

"Come on! Come on! Come on! I almost got it."

Whenever I'm in thinking mode or I'm concentration I put my tongue over the top of my bottom lip.

"There it goes, I'm almost there."

Click! I did it!

I looked at my watch and the time read 4:30 am. OOOOHHHH Shit! I hurried to the living room and took my clothes off. I placed them under the couch and got a glass of ice water. I then began to mess up my hair up to make it look old and then proceeded up the stairs. As I was unlocking the door to my room my uncle opened up his door. He scared the hell out of me.

"Good morning Face, what you doing up this early," he says.

"My throat was dry so I went to get something to drink."

"Do you mind getting me some," he asked.

"Yes, I'll get it," I responded happily.

I'm not even worried about him seeing me in my underwear ''cause he's my uncle and I've lived with him since I was seven or eight years old. Then I remembered that I just had sex for the first time and was experiencing some bleeding. So instead of turning around I decided to grab my robe and then go back downstairs to get his water. I placed the ice in the cup and then began to fill it with water. All I could see was the reflection of the dawn of the day approaching. I turned the water off and went back upstairs to give him his water. I knocked on his door, gave him his water and went to my room. I finally sat on my own bed and just took time out to say thank you Jesus for saving me. I need to take a bath so I can get all of this filth off me. My vagina sure does hurt. It feels like a pole was shoved up in me. All I want to do is get cleaned up and go to sleep, but I can't do anything until my uncle leaves.

This shit is throbbing or is my heart beating down there? I wish I could talk to my mother about what I just did, but she don't care. She's too busy getting high. I quickly changed my thoughts when I heard the door shut. I jumped up and ran into the bathroom to start my bath water. While the water was running I looked in the mirror and began to cry. I couldn't believe I just had sex with this dude. I am so scared to see him again. I was in the tub soaking for a long time. I scrubbed myself and got out of the tub. I hear a knock at the door.

"Who is it?" I ask.

"It's me girl, open the door!" It was my oldest sister.

Damn, this hating ass girl gets on my nerves.

"What are you doing up this early?" She asked.

"It's too hot in my room so I took a bath to cool off," I responded.

I realize I didn't wash my panties out, so I decided to do it then. My nosey ass sister starts asking me all these dumb ass questions when she supposed to just be going to the bathroom. She asks did my period come on. I said yes and left it at that 'cause I sure wasn't going to tell her my business so she could tell grandmom on me. I grabbed my wet panties and walked down the hall to my room. I peeked into grannies room, but she was still sleep, just like I'm going to be in a matter of minutes.

I lie down in my bed and wonder if Nikki made it in the house safely. I'll find out later. It sure felt good to lie down and before I knew it I was fast asleep.

The phone is ringing. I was so tired I didn't even bother to answer the phone. Then I hear "Trina! Trina!, pick up the phone."

"Who is it?" I asked.

"It's somebody named Freddy."

Full of excitement I hurried up out the bed and grabbed the phone. "What's up Shorty, what you doing?" asked Freddy.

"Hey Freddy, I'm not doing anything. Then he asked if he could see me again. I said, "Yes, but not at night. This time we would have to meet during the day 'cause I wasn't trying to get myself in trouble."

"I'm not trying to get you in trouble Boo" he says. Then he asked me was last night my first time or was he just too big for me. I asked why and he said because I was acting like it was. Embarrassed, I responded, "Please, I can handle you, don't even blow your head up. I was just uncomfortable last night 'cause my cousin and your friend were there."

"Ok, we'll see," he says.

"Whatever!" I whispered.

"So what time can I see you?"

"Around eight," I said and then we hung up.

It's about five o'clock; I opened the front door to see whose outside before I start my daily chores. The sun was shining and the wind was slightly blowing, the neighbors were out on their steps watching the kids play rope and ride their bikes.

"Hi Ms. Edna," I yelled.

"Hello Trina," she says.

Ms. Edna was the type of lady who spoiled her children and kept a real nice house with all the up to date furniture. She's light brown skin with long Indian hair and China eyes and full lips. Oh and let's not forget her dimples. That's my baby; whenever I needed someone to talk to she was always there.

My grandmom is calling me so I shut the door and went to see what she wanted. First she asked me did I clean the downstairs yet and I answered no. Then she says well go to the store and get some Ajax, bleach, pine sol and a Pepsi.

"Can I have a dollar?"

"Yeah and tell Tina to clean the bathroom."

"Ok!" And out the door I went.

My grandmom didn't have the most up to date furniture in her house, but what she did have she took good care of. My grandmom was all I had so I did whatever she asked, even if I didn't really want to. She takes care of everybody, even those that are less fortunate than us. I considered us to be the less fortunate, but grandmom would always say God is good. There is always someone worse off than us.

I got everything grandmom wanted from the store and just as I am leaving I run into Nikki.

"What up freak?"

"Hey girl!" I extend my hand to smack hers, but instead she grabbed my hand and pulled me close to her.

"Girl, do you know that Freddy is eighteen years old? "

"No! I thought he was about our age."

"Well he's not!"

"How do you know?"

"Tommy told me he's a freak and likes young girls."

That's the second time I heard that I said to myself.

"Girl, that dick was so good!" Nikki says.

"It was?" I said with a shocked look on my face.

"Wait, how did you know where I was? I asked.

"I called and Aunt Linda told me."

Nikki whispered, "girl this nigga ate me out and I sucked his dick." I almost dropped the bags, she took it to another level, I thought. "Then we did it on the dresser with my legs wrapped around his back. Girl, I can still feel it," she says.

"Shut the hell up girl, you are lying!" I was just mad "cause my first time didn't go that smooth.

"So why didn't you come out early like you always do?" I asked, "cause I'm on punishment, I lied and told my mom that you had my money in your pocket from last night in a jacket you let me hold. She said I could go and come right back. So can I have $3.50 until my dad gives me some money? I'll give it back after church tomorrow."

"You better!" I say as I give her the money.

"Let me go before she add another week to my punishment," Nikki says as she walks out the door.

"Grandmom, I'm back!"

"Alright put my change up until I come down."

I quickly started cleaning because I knew I had a date and I really wanted things to look and smell good. It took about an hour and a half to finish cleaning. I took a shower, got dressed and went in the room with my grandmom.

"Are you done everything? She asked.

Yes, I replied.

What time did you get in last night?

'Cause I waited up for you, she said.

I came home after the party was over.

And what time was that?

One thirty, I replied.

Did I say you could stay out that late? Don't make me stop you from going ok?

Yes, I said with a sad look on my face. That look got her every time. Who's this boy that kept calling all day while you were sleep? His name is Freddy. Can he please come over for a while I asked? Out of nowhere here comes the hater, my oldest sister. Saying, don't let him come over grandma. She's too young for a boyfriend. I gave her a look that would kill. She rolled her eyes at me and grabbed her sneaks and left. She really didn't care what grandma's answer would be just as long a she threw salt in the game. He can stay for a while, granny said. But remember you have church tomorrow and you also have to sing. T hank you granny I say. He'll be here around eight. Give me my change, I didn't forget and get me a glass of ice please. I did just that and then went to sit out on the steps.

I was bored that I got the girls on the block together so that we could step. It was China, Rhonda, Taresa , Ashley and me. I'm always the leader in something because that's just what I do. Spread out everyone, I say. We're in place then I walk to the back. 1, 2, 3, Mississippi Hit It, Clap, Hit it. Then with a loud scream, "Yo Ashley! Spell Mississippi right now. You can take my M, My I, My Crooked Letter Crooked Letter I , My Humpback, Humpback I." Then it was my turn and so on and so on.

The next team came up and they did this step called, "Look Bitch." They came back hard. So we had to come back even harder. This time we had to curse because they cursed. Our step was called "Looking At the Front Door." It was my turn and I walked straight up to this girl face with my pointer finger in her face without touching her with a fake attitude and said, "Looking, looking at my door all I see is this black whore....." That's when I see him riding up on a bike. I made my way back to my spot to finish up. It was their turn next and I quit and walked with him as he rode the bike. We sat on the steps and talked for a while, and then Terry walked up and said, "We won, even though you left."

"What's up Freddy?" she said. "Did you see my brother at the courts today?"

"No I didn't go today." He responded.

As he was talking I noticed his tooth was missing and I didn't like that, but I quickly shook that off 'cause besides his missing tooth he had the whole package. It was getting dark and Ashley went home. We were finally alone. Everyone went inside except us. It felt like we knew each other for a long time. He walked up to me and wrapped his arms around my neck giving me a hug.

"Baby, I miss you!" He started kissing my lips, sliding his tongue down my throat in a forcing way. He then began to grab my butt.

"Stop Freddy, don't do this out here." I say. When we went in the house and sat down on the couch to watch television. My uncle came home a little after 10 pm. He looked straight at me and said, "Who's this young man?"

"His name is Freddy." I replied.

"How are you doing young man, I'm Uncle Tommy." He shook his hand and looked him in the eyes and said, "I expect you out of here in the next hour."

"Yes," Freddy replied as my uncle walked up the stairs. Freddy flagged him and started rubbing my legs.

I don't know what it is but I just melt in his presence. He pushed open my legs and laid me back on the sofa and started grinding on me like crazy. Oh my God! This boy has a big dick that makes me want more of it the bigger it gets.

"Stop Freddy, I might get caught!"

"Shhh, I'll stop before they come down."

I lay there letting him suck and lick my breast like he was expecting milk to come out. Then he slid my shorts to the side and placed his fingers on my clit rubbing it up and down in a fast motion. I started moving back because this time it felt better than the first time. He's nasty I think to myself as he slid his fingers in his moth to wet them again this time pushing them in and out of my vagina. I'm soaking wet and ready so I think.

"You like this shit don't you? He asked."

"Yes," I said with my eyes halfway closed. Trying to stay focused on what's going on and what's about to happen.

"Oh shit I'm about to cum. Wait! Let me lick it first." He said, placing my shorts on the side of the couch and my legs in the air. I started shaking like crazy. Just then he slid his dick in my vagina. This time he only put the head in and it didn't hurt that bad. We tried to be as quiet as possible. This pussy is tight. I like it like this tight and juicy," He said.

"Wait Freddy somebody's coming!"

He jumped up and pushed his dick back in his pants, zipped them up and sat down. I grabbed my shorts, slid them on, sat down and pretended we were talking the whole time. I forgot that he comes down to make sure the doors and windows are locked. I looked at Freddy and motioned for him to wipe his face. I leaned over and wiped the rest he missed.

"Young man it's time for you to leave," said Uncle Tommy. We walked to the door and whispered in my ear, "You owe me."

I locked the door after he left and ran to the window to watch him walk down the street until he was out of eyesight.

It's Sunday morning and I hear "Marry Mason" on the radio.

My grandma sends me to the store for stockings for both of us. I get them and hurry back home to get dressed "cause church start at 10:45 am sharp. "How come Tina doesn't have to go to church?" I asked.

"Because she's mean and I don't feel like arguing with her now let's go our ride is outside.

I made it to the back just in time before the choir started marching. We sang two songs and then the pastor got up to preach. I began to feel funny about the things I was doing behind my grandma's back. Tears began to fall. The time went by fast. The tithes were collected and church was dismissed. I always feel better after church about life and whatever it may bring. I know it will be all right. Grand mom and I went out to lunch and then went home to prepare for the next day. She was always so organized. She would say, "Why put off tomorrow what you can do today."

I thought to myself, and thanked God for her "cause she's the only one who truly loves me for me.

Tina was home downstairs blasting the radio listening to that devil's juice. I can truly say going to church every Sunday made a big difference on some of the decisions I made because If I could get away with murder, this girl would be the second on the list, with my mom being in first place. Deep down I truly love them both but I wished that they would change.

My sister hates me and I don't know why. Truth be told I'm her biggest fan. She's a straight A student and She's on the swimming team, basketball team, and baseball team. And on top of all that she's the oldest, which makes her the boss. But she's too dumb to know it.

"Big Nose! Grandma said warm the food up that she prepared last night."

"No she didn't," I replied.

"Yes she did." as she pushed me.

"You better keep your f**king hand off me!" I say. Realizing that another thing I need to work on is my temper. I can't stand you she mumbled under her breath after I told her that I was going to ask grandma myself. Her story quickly changed.

"Baby do the dishes after supper please." Grandma often called me baby when she wanted me to do something. We ate dinner and did our chores. Now it's time for bed. I said goodnight to everyone and kissed granny on the cheek. This might sound crazy, but I have to say my prayers to ask for forgiveness for whatever I said or done throughout the course of the day. I always prayed that my grandmother would see another day. I prayed that he would kill my mom and only he knew why I prayed this prayer and then I asked for forgiveness and before long off to sleep I went.

"Good morning class," Mrs. Turner said. "Advisory is starting." While calling out our names for roll call I notice something that I have never paid any mind before. The teacher called Shannon to read. I noticed that around her neck she had a chain on with Freddy's name on it. I pushed my head back and squinted my eyes real hard to make sure I was seeing what I thought I saw. I swore I saw that same chain on Freddy on Saturday when He was at my house. I'm trying not to let my emotions get the best of me, but I can't stop the boiling in my blood. I'm trying to concentrate on my incomplete homework that was due on Friday. I quickly finished it. I gave Shannon a look she'll never forget. This girl thought she was the shit and I never liked her anyway. This had just put the icing on the cake. It was then that I realized that this chick was friend of my friend Lori. I'll see her in the hall when the bell rings I thought to myself.

The bell rang. It was time for first period class, which was English. Lori is in my class. She sat one seat behind me. I wrote her a letter asking her if Shannon was bowlegged Freddy's girl-friend. She wrote back, "Yes" and asked why I wanted to know. I responded that he and I are dating. "Oh my goodness! They have been dating for a while now. Do you know how old he is? "

"No," I said.

"Me either," she said "but I heard that he's about 18 years old." That was irrelevant at this moment "cause I was starting to feel him more now than ever. The teacher asked us to stop with the passing of paper and to do some work. We did just that!

I didn't see either one of them for the rest of the day. After school Ashley, Lori, Yvette and I walked home together. Lori plays to much some times, out of nowhere she looks at me and says "Katrina you didn't see Freddy over there walking with his arm around Shannon waist?" Ashley beat me first by saying "Where? Girl, I told you he wasn't no good!" I played it cool "cause we never said we were a couple. I'm not going to front though my feelings were crushed. We quickly caught up to them, quickly. I glanced at him with a look like I can't believe you. His eyes lit up like a Christmas tree, but it's cool I'll get him back. "

What's up Shan?"

"Hey Lori," She replied with a soft squeaky voice.

"Hey Freddy!" Ashley said.

I'm flaming now. Don't talk to him I tell her. He don't know whether to move his hand or not, so he just puts them by his side. I can see he's hoping I don't say anything. I just started walking extra fast so that I could get away from them. Before long we were back around the way. We all split and went our separate ways.

I walked in the house and my grandma was at the table crying.

"What's wrong Granny?"

"It's your mother, she came here and stole all of my meats out the fridge, now how am I going to feed y'all. She's not tak-ing from me, she's taking from y'all, her children. Sometimes I just want to give y'all back to her. "Please Granny, don't do that! She doesn't love us. Here is some money I made doing hair, you can have it." I said. It took everything out of her to take it, but I wouldn't have it any other way. She gave up everything for us. I hate that b**ch of a mother. The more I thought about how I hated her, the more anger built up inside of me for Freddy too. My grandma quickly got herself together and sent my older sister to the store for lunch meat and bread. "Thank you baby for your help," she said as she gave me a hug and told me she loved me with all her heart. I kissed her and went upstairs.

About an hour later the phone rang. This time I answered it. "Hello, may I speak to Katrina?"

"This is she."

"What's up baby?"

"Your baby was walking with you after school!" I lashed out at him as if he was my man.

"Damn baby you act like I'm your man." He said with a smirk.

"If I am then let me know and all of that can change."

"F*ck it, then you are and at the end of the night I better have that chain!"

"Alright," He said.

The answer he gave nearly blew me away. I'm on a roll now. "I don't feel like talking now so call me when you're on your way."

"Ok," he said and we hung up the phone.

I did my homework and took a bath. While in the tub I carefully thought of what I was going to say. Dam life's a b**ch and I'm living in it. I got out of the tub and dried off. I grabbed my robe, looked in the mirror, smiled and side but thank you Lord for letting me see another day. I walked pass my sister and grandma's room quickly hoping they did not see me, knowing that if they did I would have to stop and listen to what they had to say. When I reached my room I dropped my robe, grabbed the lotion off the dresser and stood in the mirror admiring my young voluptuous body. I squeezed some lotion in my hands and began to rub them together; I slowly rubbed my hands in a circular motion over each one of my breasts. I didn't intend for this to happen, it was a mistake, but I liked the feeling I felt when the lotion and the cool air hit the tip of my nipples. I continued giving it a quick swirl with a gentle slide of the hand down to the tip of my nipple, with a gentle pull. I looked down at my legs, I'm happy with those. I reached down and slowly massaged them starting at the beginning of my thigh ending at the bottom of my feet. I l slowly turned around just to see what it looked liked from behind. I liked what I saw as I glanced back at me. Not feeling like that goody two shoe girl I used to be. Maybe it's the fact that I had some dick that makes me act this way. I liked it and I own it. They can takes this shit or leave it. I gave myself a hard smack on the butt cheek and quickly snapped out of it. Let me hurry up. I grabbed my pajamas and got dressed. I sat with granny for the rest of the day.

There was a knock on the door and before I could say a word, Tina was at the door yelling out who is it. Yes! That's the ignorant way she would constantly open the door. EEEWWWW!

"Freddy! What the hell are you doing knocking at my door?" Before he could answer I stepped down off the steps and grabbed him by the hand and we both left her standing there with this dumb ass look plastered on her face.

"I'm not your friend I said mumbling through my teeth. He grabbed me with both hands by my waist and whispered in my ear, I'm your man now and your my girl as he licked my ear I pulled away and held out my hand with my head tilted to the side and one eyebrow raised.

"Give me the chain." He reached behind his back after smacking my hand down. He then pulled me close to him and said that

I better stop acting like that. Turn around he demanded as he turned my back towards him and placed that same chain on my neck to show me that I was this new found love.

He didn't get to stay long "cause my uncle and my sister came down stairs together, young man how old is you? "Excuse me." Freddy said. You heard him. He's either 17 or 18, Tina said.

"Are you young man?" My uncle asked.

"Yes sir I am." Freddy replied.

"Do you know how old she is? He asked.

"No, I don't sir." They are talking as if I'm not even here.

"She's thirteen! I want you to leave my house and never return again," as he signaled with his hand for Freddy to leave. Now I am the one standing there with the dumb ass look on my face, while Tina smiles at me as I watch my new man walk out of the door. I walked pass Tina and said, "I hate you b**ch, you just mad because my boyfriend looks better than yours!", as I bumped her.

"Wait a minute Trina! I need to have a few words with you," my uncle said. Oh my god here come this long speech. To my surprise this time it was short, but not sweet.

"Don't let me see you with that man again or I'll break your face, understand?"

"Yes," I replied as I sucked my teeth and walked away. I went up to my room and slammed my door.

"Shit!" I hope they don't think this is going to stop me from seeing him. I'll see him on the other side of the projects. I turned off the light, said my prayers and fell asleep.

On my way to school the next day, my squad and I were walking to school together. This particular day we didn't wait for Ashley 'causes most of the time she would make us late so we left her. I saw Shannon and her girls on their way to school also. Lori, being the person she is gave Shannon a shout out. "What's up girl?"

"Nothing," she says. While Lori has her back turned I pulled the zipper down on my spring jacket to show off Freddy's chain. If looks could kill, I would have died right there. I smiled at her as she stared at me in hopes that she would step so that I could pull out her long pretty hair. I thought she wouldn't say anything. We reached our school, Fitz Simon Jr. High. The bell was about to ring so we said our goodbyes and gave our hugs while others rolled their eyes. I can feel it's about to be beef.

I'm in my class now just about to settle down when this boney ass girl name Stephanie, walks up in my face and whispered b**ch don't test me, I'll beat your ass all up in this place." The teacher yelled, "Girls settle down before I throw both of you out of this class."

I sat down in my chair after I gave that girl a stare and said, "Bitch I'm a whip that ass and you can bet a dollar on my very word."

"Whatever hoe, bring it," she mumbled under her breath hoping I didn't hear her.

The class settled down after the teacher began to run the chalk back and forth across the board. After regaining control of the class, she pulled out the roll sheet and began taking roll. But before she could finish the bell rang. I grabbed my things with the quickness because this girl had just made my day. I walked out the class and stood right beside the classroom door. Now Shannon wants to walk all slowly. Let me see how much mouth this bitch has now I said out loud. I waited impatiently for her to come out. A small crowd was forming, not noticing that her friends were standing in the crown listening to what the crowd was saying. They made their way to the front and one of them yelled out come on "Shan" I got your back. So I turned around and said out of frustration, "Well then you can get this ass whooping that Shan's about to get bitch!"

Before I knew it I was fighting her friend. I grabbed her by her hair just as soon as she got within arm reach. Her face was all I wanted to hit. I'm not going to lie, she gave me a run for my money, but after I finished with her face, I didn't need amybody to tell me who won or lost that fight. The dean came so fast and gripped the both of us up. We didn't know what hit us. When I realized that I was in the office, all that tough shit I was talking came to a complete halt. I looked at this girl whom I had no beef with, staring in my face with her hair standing all over her head. She began cracking her knuckles to let me know this wasn't over with. "What's your name young lady and your phone number?" The dean asked.

"I'm not giving your anything while she's standing there. She'll never play on my phone." Before I would give him any of my information he took Shan in another room. I then gave him my home number and mothers name and before I could get her name out good tears started running down my face. I tried to explain that I didn't know how I started fighting ''cause I wasn't arguing with her, it was her friend who I had beef with. "Stephanie tried to be super save a hoe and jumped in it and got her ass whooped."

"You better watch your mouth," Mr. Brown yelled while he was in the middle of dialing my number.

"Hello." I couldn't hear who answered the phone but by the looks on his face he must of spoke with my mother. "Thanks you Lawrence," was all I heard.

"I'll be sending her home in a hour; do you want me to let her leave by herself or you're coming to get her?"

I assume she said send her home with the pink slip.

"Ok, have a nice day." Mr. Brown said before hanging up.

"Here young lady, take these home, get your things out of your locker and I'll escort you to the front door. Don't return until you have a parent with you."

"Shit!" Oh my god I'm a get my ass kicked was all I could think about after leaving school. I guess they'll send Stephanie home after I leave.

What the f*ck was I thinking when I gave that man my real number. I'm going to kick Shannon ass for all the pain she's causing in my life. I bet she's glad it wasn't her face I scratched up. Old light skinned b**ch. As I finally reached my block I started thinking did I hear Mr. Brown clear when he said Mrs. Lawrence or did she say Lewis. I'll soon find out. I turned the knob to the door when the door opened up by itself.

"Get the f*ck in here you little bastard!" Is what that f**king poor excuse of a mother said out of her filthy ass mouth.

"You like fighting in school? Your ass is in the house until I say you can breathe on the other side of this door," pointing at my forehead while she yelled. "I should break your ass in half b**ch." A name she called me on a regular. I didn't even respond because I hated the to be in the same space as her. I hate this f*cking lady was all I thought as I stood in front of her the whole time she talked. I thought to myself what the hell is she mad for? It isn't like she sends me to school or like she's going to be the one who'll take me back. Not totally hearing the question she just asked me ''cause I was blocking her out. She asked it again. Your sister Tina, told me that you're messing with Freddy from Tabor Street. That's the last time I'm going to ask you is this true? I'm scared now ''cause this lady is crazy. That's why we're not living with her now. Should I say yes or no? I decided to say yes.

"Are you having sex yet? Tell me the truth, I won't be mad," she said. I waited for a minute and said, yes. Out of now where she pulls out the extension cord and began to beat me like a runaway slave. She kicked me, pulled my hair, stepped on my stomach and called me all kinds of whores. I'm falling into the refrigerator, running down the hall crying out for my grandmother's help.

"Grandma, grandma please make her stop. My grandma grabbed the cord and held on tight to the other end of the cord making sure that was the last swing.

"You can't be beating that girl like that just 'cause she's suspended," grandma said.

"This little b**ch is out here f*cking grown men!" My mom said. If you were around more she wouldn't be doing it, she would have known better grandma said as she turned around and saw the blood dripping from my legs and my face. "Baby, go clean yourself up." I could see the anger in her eyes as I walked away in pain. From a distance I could still hear my mom and grandma arguing. Get the hell out of my house Cindy before I call the police grandma yelled at the top of her lungs. "You're not supposed to be around these kids anyway."

"Who the f*ck is going to keep me away? That's mine up there. I can do whatever the f*ck I want to do."

I didn't believe it when granny said she would call the police. I guess granny doesn't make idol threats 'cause not to long after that the cops were knocking at the door.

"It's the cops for you," Cindy said.

"What's the problem ma'am?"

"All I want y'all to do is to make her leave."

"Does she live here?"

"No!" Granny said.

"I'm about to leave. I don't even know why she called y'all, old evil witch," she said while packing her bag.

"Officer she's not to be within 50 feet of her children. She damn near beat her daughter to death," Granny said. Then the officer asked could he see me. Just as the officer was finishing his sentence Tina walked in.

"What's going on?"

"Just go and get your sister," Granny said.

"Katrina, Grandmom want you! What happened to you? She got a nerve to ask."

"It's because of you and your big mouth!"

"What I do?"

"You told on me about Freddy!" I said while pouring peroxide on the cuts that occurred during my beating.

"Come here baby," Granny yelled up the steps. I slowly walked down the steps with my hands on my belly.

"See what she did?" Granny showed the officer my cuts.

"If she returns call me and I'll be right back to lock her up Ma'am," the officer said as he gave her a pink piece of paper. Granny walked him to the door and told the officer to have a great day.

Baby we're not going to talk right now, but we'll talk about this later Granny said. She took me in the living room to do a complete check up from the neck up.

"You'll be ok," she said. "Go upstairs to your room and think about why you got suspended from school."

I walked away wishing it would have been this easy if Granny had answered the phone first. Then again, I love her too much to have Granny mad at me. I wonder if I'm still on punishment. Damn I got my ass whooped. My body and my mind was hurt. I laid in my bed wondering if this dude was really worth it. I think I'm going to leave him alone. Shit the thrill is gone anyway or so I thought. All this shit I'm going through and he haven't even given me money yet. He'll pay for this I thought to myself and that b**ch Shannon, I'll get her when I see her on the streets. She can't hide, we both live in the projects. Diamond World is another name we call North Side Projects.

There's a knock on my door.

"Who is it?"

"It's Tina, can I come in for a minute?"

"NO!" I yelled, "Get away from my door, I can't stand you!"

"Y'all cut it out!" Grandma screamed, that made her walk away from my bedroom door. I laid on the bed, looking at the ceiling with nothing to do.

Why do my mom hate me so much God? Why doesn't my dad want anything to do with me, my brother and sisters? God how come you gave that lady ten child that she won't take care of? God I know that Granny says you do everything for a reason, but what's my reason for living? Why couldn't I have a loving family? What's wrong with me? How come my sister hates me? She's always starting something. I don't even have a relationship with her and she's the only blood that's left in the same house with me out of my moms' kids. I wiped the tears from my face and began to wonder why I was ever born, I wouldn't have such a crappy life. I should commit suicide, but it might hurt too much. Maybe I'll take some pills. Yeah! That's what I'll do. Now I'm thinking about how I can get to my grandma's medicine. I'll get it when she goes to sleep tonight. My body hurts so bad, I'll just stay in the bed until dinner was the last thought I remember having before falling into a deep sleep.

Being awakened by my Grandma nearly startled me.

"Is it time for dinner?"

"Dinner," Granny said, it's morning. You wouldn't get up so I decided to let you sleep. Get up, wash your face and brush your teeth so that we can talk before I leave."

I got up and did as I was told. I could smell the aroma of coffee in the air as I made my way to the dining room.

"Have a seat." Granny motioned for me to sit. I guess this is what she does in the morning before leaving. Grandma had coffee and a corn muffin and I had the same. She sat down and looked me straight in the eyes and asked me what happened in school yesterday. It was something about Grandma. I just couldn't lie to her if I tried.

"So that's it?" She asked, "You're telling me that you're fighting over a boy!"

"No!" I said.

"But you are," Granny replied. "If that boy is truly your boyfriend, in which you're too young for, you wouldn't be having this problem now."

"But I am...." is all I could get out before she interrupted. "No man is worth fighting for, If you miss one bus you just go on and catch the next one."

For some strange reason I understood what she was saying. "You never let them see you sweat. Let him go and if he understands that you're too young, when you get older, he'll return if it's meant to be. Besides, you're too young to be out here giving your body away. If you keep allowing him to milk the cow for free, there won't be any left for your husband when you get older. Now give me a hug and a kiss. I love you and I need you to help me keep this house in order while I go and see a man about a dog." Meaning she was on her way to work.

"I love you Grandma," I reminded her as she grabbed her things to leave. "Have a nice day!" I told her as I shut the door. I gave a quick look to the sky and said, Lord you are so slick. That's why you made me oversleep, so that you could show me that there is someone who loves me, my Granny. I'm glad I didn't get a chance to take her pills I thought to myself as I began to clean up our mess. I can't wait to see Freddy; it's over with us. I'll break up with him after I get off punishment and when I see Shannon, only God knows what's going to happen.

Time flew by so fast. I haven't seen Freddy in a while. Come to think of it, I haven't seen my mom either. Nothing has changed with my sister. She's still hateful, but I just ignore her.

"Uncle Tommy, if I clean your room for you could I have some money?"

He shook his head yes and gave me instructions on exactly how he wanted his room cleaned. I made a quick ten dollars for the party. I'm in, I say to myself. I have my party money and my get high money. I'll see Nikki tonight 'cause she's off her punishment today. I got dressed after doing all of my chores. Uncle Tommy reminded me not to stay out late or I'd be back on punishment. Let me call Squirrel, that's Nikki's nickname. When I called Nikki, her mom answered the phone. It was loud noises in the background, so I could hardly hear her.

"Hello, is Nikki there?" I asked.

"Yeah, hold on."

"Hello, hey cousin, are you going to the Dollar Holla tonight?"

"Where?"

"On 22nd Street, I think it's at Ms. Pat's house."

"Oh yes. It's on and popping." She said.

"Alright let me get dressed."

"What are you wearing? She asked.

"I'm wearing my black and red Adidas sweat suit and my black and red paten leather Adidas sneakers."

"Well I'll wear my blue and white suit with blue and white shell tops."

Alright, see you later."

We both hung up. Sometimes Nikki play too much, she'll ask me what I'm wearing and then change up on me.

Well let me go to the phone booth and call Freddy. I gave myself one more spray of my sunflower perfume before leaving.

I've tried to call him all day, but there was no answer. I'll try one more time before I take this long walk to Ashley's house.

I'm now standing on the corner of 22nd Street. I spot a public phone so I decide to call him one last time.

"Hello, oh my goodness Freddy, I've been calling you for a while."

"I heard about you fighting," he said.

"Yeah and that's why I'm calling you." I paused for a moment and took a deep breath. "I don't want to be your girl anymore. It's over," I said.

"What you say girl?" I could tell this came as a surprise. We're not breaking up! You are my girl and we're staying together," he said in a loud angry voice. "Look Katrina, I'll talk to you later and then he hung up the phone. Sill standing there with the phone in my hand I decided to hang up and walk away.

The boys are out tonight playing ball in the high field. In the corner some of them were playing dice and from the looks of things Chub looked angry. I hope they don't start fighting and shooting while I'm out here. I noticed Shannon and her girls sitting on the pole. I walked pass them hoping that one of them would jump. I had a quick flashback of the conversation I had with granny and decided to keep moving while watching my back at the same time. I don't know what she heard, but she didn't even lift her head when I passed by her. I guess the beef is over, I thought! It's never a dull moment around the PJ's, that's why I love it.

Finally, I arrived at Terry's house. She wasn't home so I sat my black ass down on her steps until she came home. When she came home, she brought the whole crew with her. We greeted each other and went inside. We had a good time as usual. I got so high the room was spinning. I began to throw up at the table so one of my homie's took me to the grass out back.

"You alright Shawn asked."

"I feel better now," I said and we both went back into the house.

"It's party time y'all let's roll."

"Hold up I mumbled, I have to call Nikki."

She didn't answer so we left. We were so high that we sang

songs while we walked. We even started bussing on each other without getting mad. That's just how we play in the hood.

"Damn y'all, that line is long", Yvette said. "This joint must be packed!"

We made it to the front in no time. It was like all the teens in the projects were here. We danced and talked shit to the guys we didn't know. All of my girlfriends looked ok so it didn't' take us long to get the phone numbers.

I met this guy name Wayne. He looked even better than Freddy, I thought as we exchanged numbers.

"You're wearing that sweat suit?" he said.

"Thank you", I said.

"I'm sure I know you from somewhere," he said.

"If I would've seen you before I would've remembered your face," I said.

This dude was brown skin with curly hair. He was kind of on the tall side, with beautiful eyes. They way he dressed complimented him well. He had a cool walk and he could have anyone in this party and he chose me. The DJ started playing slow songs and he asked me if I wanted to dance. I accepted. We danced to "I'll Call Your Name" by switch.

Damn he smells good, I thought as we grinded on each other to the music. I laid my head on his shoulder in an effort to try and stop the room from spinning. His hands are on my butt. He's gently massaging it and it feels good. Suddenly, I feel a tap on my shoulder and I look up and to my surprise it's Freddy.

"Come here," he says, after he says what's up to Wayne.

"What's up Freddy, this your girl?"

"No!" I said answering for Freddy.

"What?" Freddy said. I took his chain out of my pocket and tried to hand it to him, but instead of taking the chain he grabbed my arm and twisted it while leading me through the crowd.

"Get off of me Freddy," I yelled. "I don't go with you anymore!"

My friends were too busy having fun they didn't notice me leaving.

"Girl you think I'm playing with you," he said, as if I was a child.

"Freddy I'm not going with you, let me go!"

When we made it pass the crowd to the outside that's when the real Freddy showed up.

Before I could speak he slapped the holy hell out of me. I was seeing stars. Once I got myself together we fought like a cat and a dog. As you already know, he won. I stood outside crying ''cause deep down I really liked Freddy, but he was causing me too much pain. I guess he felt bad ''cause he apologized and said it would never happen again.

He wiped my eyes and wrapped his arms around me and started slowly grinding on my butt. I know he doesn't think he's getting any after treating me like this. We sat under the ramp of 09 building for about an hour before he talked me into going with him to his friend house. We got on the elevator. It was just Freddy and I. I'm not talking much, but he is. He's very aggressive I thought to myself. I'll pretend I'm his friend, but when I leave I'm gone for good. This nigga wants to put his hands on me. I can show him better than I could tell him, ''cause he doesn't seem to be listening.

We made it. As the elevator door opened I could smell the urine from the hallway. Before exiting the elevator he pulled the key from his pocket. He opened the door and said, "sit right there and I'll be back." He walked to the backroom and it took him a minute to return.

"Come here! I got up and walked towards him . He didn't waste any time taking off his pants. He undid mine as he stood in front of me completely naked. He took one of my hands to stroke his dick. That thing grew so fast.

"Freddy," I said, trying to get his attention. "I don't want to do it."

"Yes you do," he replied grabbing me closer to him. He began French kissing me and rubbing my nipples. I'm not going to help him get his shit off, I thought. I lay completely still trying not to move. He slid the head of his penis in my vagina easy this time. It didn't hurt that much. Before I knew it, I was taking the whole dick.

"Turn over," he said. I wouldn't so he grabbed my legs and twisted them at the ankles making me turn over. He's banging my back out, slapping me on the ass.

"Oh shit! Oh shit! This pussy is mine," he said. "Is this my pussy?" Fuck no, I said in my mind, but was to afraid to say it aloud.

"It's yours," I said as he's moving faster and faster. He is about to cum. I noticed he didn't wear a condom when he pulled his dick out and started ejaculating between my butt cheeks. He slid his dick back and forth until he was completely finished. We didn't even get up this time to rush and get washed and dressed. He lay behind me and fell asleep. I dozed off until my high was completely gone. All I could think about was getting home. "

Freddy! Freddy! Wake Up! I have to get home before my uncle gets up for work and notice I'm not home."

We both got up and went in the bathroom. He gave me a rag and got one for himself and we cleaned ourselves up. It's 2:30 in the morning, I hope I can make it in the house without getting in trouble. As we walked towards my house, Freddy told me that he didn't want to catch me in another dude face again. He also said he took the number that I had in my pocket. We stopped at the end of my block, said our goodbyes and he watched me open the door to my house before leaving. I tip toed up the steps and went in my room, took my clothes off and fell asleep.

You'll never believe what my eyes are seeing. Is that Freddy! Could that be him with another female? This chick is dark skinned, skinny with short hair. I can't see her face so I decided to get a closer look. I think it's his sister but I'm not sure. It's only one way to find out. He's supposed to be my man, so I walked up on him from behind and gave him a hug. If you could have seen the look on his ugly chicks face when I did that!

"What's up Boo," I said to Freddy trying to be smart.

"Oh shit!" he says followed by "hey girl" as if we were just street friends.

"Freddy, who the fuck is this little girl?" she asked.

"That's just my friend," he responded.

"Oh now I'm just your friend. I'm tired of arguing with these bitches over you Freddy," I said.

"First of all I have been dealing with Freddy for five years," she responded. That shit blew my mind when she said that. "Well, where the fuck was you when Freddy and I were having sex? Because he has been beating this pussy up! I finished the last word and turned and looked at Freddy. His ass was mad now because this chick decides to walk up on me. Just as she went to swing I ducked and followed up with a two piece to the face. Freddy grabbed me and his sister grabbed her. I smacked Freddy because my feelings were hurt. It felt like somebody had stabbed me in the heart. He's trying to explain to me that what I think I see is not really what's happening.

"I guess she's your main girl huh?" I asked. "You have a lot of nerves Freddy, you damn near beat me the fuck up a couple of weeks ago for just dancing and now I find out that you had a girlfriend for five years!"

"Wait!" He says. "She's my sister's best friend, I'm always going to see her even if we breakup! She is a friend of the family."

"Here Freddy," I snatched his chain off and threw it. "I'm

done with you," I said as I walked away. His sister walked behind Freddy saying, "Kitta said, if you don't come on she's locking her doors and you can get your shit downstairs in front of 09 Building." Hearing that, it stopped me in my tracks.

"You mean to tell me that you fucked me in her house!" I asked. After hearing what I said, that bitch went off on him. That was my opportunity to get the hell out of this fucked up relationship. I kept walking and this time and never looked back.

It's been weeks since I last seen Freddy. I miss him, but life goes on. I haven't been to church in a while. The more I party, the less they see me in the house of the Lord. Why do I feel like I'm missing something in my life, I kept asking myself.

I decided to go to the hair store and stock up on my hair supplies. AS I am bending down to get some gel, I feel these big hands cover my eyes.

"Who's this?" grabbing the tips of their fingers. I turned around to see who it was. It was him that handsome dude I met at the party. Why haven't you called me yet?" He asked. While trying to come up with a good excuse, he asked.

"Was that your man?"

"Who's Freddy?"

"No, Freddy," he responded trying to be smart.

"We're not together anymore," I said."

"Good, so call me, use the number I gave you."

"Freddy took it and threw it away," I said.

I want to touch his hair so bad while he's standing in front of me looking so good. After talking for about ten minutes, we paid for our supplies and left the store.

"I'll call you," he said as he walked away.

"What time," I asked, 'cause I sure didn't want to miss this bus, as my grandmother would say.

When I got in the house I'll call Nikki to see if we can do

something this weekend. It completely slipped my mind. I've been playing the game sorry with my grandmom for so long, that time went right by. "This is my last game granny," I said as she made her way around the board sending my only man back to start. "Sorry! I won!" she yelled. I helped her put the games away and picked up the phone to call Nikki.

"Hello is Nikki home Aunt Sarah?"

"No, she's spending the weekend at her father's house."

"Ok," I said as I hung up the phone. I'll call Quine, maybe we can hook up I said as I dialed his number. I took a quick look at the time. It's 8 o'clock, if I catch him early maybe he'll see me early. He picked up the phone on the third ring.

"Hello," he says.

"Hello can I speak to darrell?"

"This is he, who is this?"

This is Katrina."

"So you finally called? What's up," he asked.

"You're what's up, I'm trying to see you tonight."

Completely surprised and caught off guard he replied, "Damn girl you're straight to the point!"

Not noticing since I've been with Freddy, I've changed a lot.

"So what's up? Can I see you or not I asked?"

Hoping he'd say yes.

"What time," he asked.

"How about ten o'clock," I said.

"I'll be there. I'll meet you at Lucky's Garden Chinese Store. Don't have me waiting long."

"I won't," I said before hanging up the phone.

I had a hour and a half before I could leave to meet him. I already knew I was going to fuck him that night. I took a bubble bath and soaked my pussy good before getting out of the tub. I lotion my body, then ran back in the bathroom to brush my teeth. I turned the radio on and listened to some music while I pressed my hair out. My hair is about shoulder length so it took me a while to finish. I put on some tight jeans that made my butt look extra big, a pink polo shirt and a pair of white high top Reeboks sneakers. I sprayed myself down with perfume. I placed my money in my pockets and put on my figure eight earrings. I locked my bedroom door and went to give granny a goodnight kiss to find out what time I had to be back in the house.

"Twelve," she says before sitting down in here lounge chair

"Granny, I'm leaving," I yelled.

"Be careful she say," always whenever I'm leaving the house.

"I will," I said as I made my way down the steps. The store was right across the street from my house. He was standing there waiting just like he said. It was kind of crowded at the store. People were outside waiting for their food. I walked up to him looking real good.

"You ready, we're going to my house," he said as we were walking.

I don't like young boys anymore. I don't have time to teach them shit about how to please me. We walked about three blocks to get to his house.

"We're here," he said as he walked up the steps.

"Is your mom home?" I asked.

"Yes, but she's upstairs. I'm a grown man."

"And what do you mean by grown?"

"I'm eighteen years old."

"Oh I can handle him," I mumbled.

He has a nice ass. I patted his ass trying to get a free feel. His room is the truth. I can see he likes basketball a lot. There were trophies all over. His bed was made nice and neat. He had burgundy and black silk sheets and nineteen inch television sitting on a stand with a stereo system underneath. He turned on the radio. He switched the bulbs in the light with red ones. I sat patiently waiting until his fine ass was finished. He didn't waste any time. He started feeling my hair and slowly kissing me on the lips. I grabbed him closer and gave him the tongue. He slid my shirt over my head and pulled out one of my breast. And with the tip of his tongue he licked my nipples like he was licking and ice cream cone. Slowly going down to my navel, he licked around it and started unbuttoning my pants. I lifted my butt up off the bed so that he could pull them off. I hope he licks the man in the boat, but he didn't. Instead he stood up in front of me and slowly rubbed that fat dick of his. I watched and waited patiently until it reached its max. I had to touch it. I placed my hand around it and rubbed it nice and slow.

"You want this big dick?"

"Yes I do," I said.

"Turn around so I can hit it from the back."

I quickly did as I was told. I bent over spreading my legs to the max. He grabbed his dick and rubbed it on my ass and slowly pushed it in my pussy. I wanted this dick bad. I threw this pussy on hike like never before. I began to take over, I rubbed his balls from underneath. This nigga is tearing me out the frame. I turned over putting my legs up in the air holding them at the ankles. He rubs my clit with one of his hands, while stroking back and forth.

"Fuck me harder," I whispered.

"You want this dick then come and get it," he said.

My hair is sweating "cause he got me working. Grabbing me by my stomach and pulling me this way and that way. I was losing my mind. Without even planning it we made sweet music together at the same time. I can't explain the power I feel when I make a man cum. I'm a pro now, I thought to myself. Completely butt naked, I didn't care if he didn't want to see me anymore. I got what I wanted. He's considering number two!

"You want to come in the bathroom with me or do you want to wait till I get out?" Feeling proud of my body, I said I'd come in with him. We took a quick shower together, got dressed and made our way back to where we met up. We said our goodbyes and gave each other a look that said it was good while it lasted. Then we went our separate ways.

I never knew that having sex was so exhausting. I made my way home, but changed my mind when I ran into Nikki. She had so much to talk about. She gave me a rundown on how much fun she has been having with Freddy's homie. I didn't want to hear anything about Freddy, so I changed the subject.

"Trina, do you think Aunt Leslie will let me stay over tonight?"

"I'll ask," I said.

Time was flying so we decided to make our way to my house. Granny was still awake when we got there.

"Why are you late?"

Without even thinking Nikki said, "Aunt Leslie she was waiting for me at my house. Will it be ok if I stayed the night?" With a straight face, she said "because Aunt Sarah is staying out tonight for all night prayer at the church."

"Next time you better call and let me know something," granny said.

"Yes Granny," I said making sure she had my undivided attention. Y'all girls go to bed and try to keep your voices down. Thanks you Aunt Leslie, Nikki said. We went to my bedroom and talked all night until we both fell asleep.

Chapter 5

I Saw Him (My Dad)

*T*his particular day, I was feeling extra happy. I just finished walking my friend Ashley to the store. I can remember the excitement that I felt racing through my body. He was walking out of the wine and spirits store with one of his best friends.

"Ashley, that's my dad right there!"

"Where?"

"He's the tall skinny guy with the curly brown hair, caramel complexion and the evil looking eyebrows. I haven't seen him in a couple of years." I don't know what to call

him. Should I call him dad or Cedric? I got myself together and managed to say, "Hi dad," as I stretched my arms wide opened to embrace him. I gave him the biggest hug ever.

"Hi baby," he said followed by a kiss on the lips. I always hated that, but what can I say it's my dad. I was trying to get every question I wanted to ask out at one time.

I asked, "where you been? Why don't you come to see me? Where are you going? Can I go?" I tried to introduce him to my friend and all he could say to me was, "I'll see you later." Then he got into the car, I waved goodbye and he waved goodbye without even asking me about my sisters and brothers. He didn't even say here's a dollar for something to drink. He just left me with a hello and a goodbye.

Ashley tried to make me feel better by saying, "girl you look just like him. You even have his nose."

I couldn't say anything, it felt like my heart just stop beating. On the way back home my attitude began to change. It was like I had a fuck it attitude all of a sudden. I told Ashley I would walk her to the rent office and then I'm going home for a while. I said my goodbyes and as I walked pass the rent office I began to cry. I couldn't believe what just happened. It was like he wasn't the same dad I used to live with. The more I thought about it, then worse I felt. I began to think if I wouldn't have seen him, he wouldn't have ever stopped pass my house. Tears rolling down my face, not caring who seen me. I began to ask God why? Why did I have to have those two people for my parents? Why don't they love me? I start to wipe my face and eyes because my tears are itching my face. I look up and I see a vision in the clouds that had me puzzled. It looked like two big hands coming out of the sky. I wiped my eyes again to make sure my eyes weren't playing tricks on me. I saw it again. It was like Jesus was telling me to come to him. I guess I was too young to understand. I quickly turned into my block and headed home, never telling anybody what I just saw.

My grandmom always makes me feel better. I went straight to her room. I don't know what it is about my granny, but she's the best medicine for a broken heart. I went in her room and sat down in the tan lounge chair and didn't say a word.

"What's wrong?" she asked. My eyes began to fill with tears.

"I just saw my dad going to the wine and spirits store with his friend. I asked him why he didn't come to see us. He just gave me a hug and said goodbye, I'll see you later and pulled off in a car. Granny," I asked. "Why don't our parents love us?" Granny responded, "But they do. They just don't know how to show it. I love you," she said as gave me a great big hug and wiped my face.

"Is that your brother and sister fighting?" We both got up, pulled back the curtain to look out the window. We stuck our heads out to see what was happening. It was my little brother Leroy crying. He noticed us looking and yelled, "the boy with the mirrors on keeps hitting me."

This boy was much bigger than him. So I went out to get my brother. I told granny I'd handle the situation. This boy is funny, I thought to myself. As I'm walking down the steps I start to chuckle ''cause my brother didn't know that those were glasses the boy was wearing, not mirrors. I went out and asked what happened. We ended it right there. My brother drives me crazy. All he does is cry and suck his thumb. He's so cute though. His complexion is dark brown. He has curly hair and light eyes. He looks more like his dad. He talks funny and is always singing some crazy song. I wiped his eyes and gave him a hug and kiss. I whispered, "I love you Leroy" in his ear and he said, "me do to." I wiped his pants and told him to go play until I called him in for dinner. "Ok," he said and ran up the block.

It's Sunday morning, grandma decided to stay home from church today. As usual granny wakes everyone up early in the morning. Nikki didn't like that.

"It's still early! It's 9:30 in the morning," Nikki said.

"That's late." I said, she usually gets us up at 9.

Uncle B-Cool was feeling good today. He made a big pot of oatmeal, toast, and orange juice for everyone. He acts like he's still in the Army and we're his little Soldiers. After breakfast Nikki went home. I cleaned the kitchen for Granny so that she could start dinner.

While I was upstairs taking a bath, Granny and Tina got started on dinner the smell of fried chicken quickly filled the air. I love

Sundays. I dried myself off and put on a pair of sweat pants and t-shirt. I love to feel comfortable and relaxed. When I made it downstairs, my sister was preparing everything for our meal. And I went to the counter to help her.

The cabbage was sitting on the table on top of the cutting board. I sat down and began cutting the cabbage. After that was done we prepared the bake macaroni and cheese. The best part was making the sweet potatoes or should I say candy yams.

It felt a little strange that my sister and I were getting along just fine. We talked about everything while we listened to Mary Mayson preach on the word of God. The last thing we made was the cornbread. I like sugar and cinnamon in the cornbread, so that's how Granny would make it, just for me. I love her so much, word just can't explain.

My Granny loves her family. She gave birth to three sets of twins. Uncle B-Cool, Uncle Jim, Aunt Tammy, Aunt Linda, Aunt Debra and Aunt Dianne (My uncles B-Cool and Jim, my aunts Tammy, Linda, Debra and Dianne) and then there is my mother Cindy. God didn't torture Granny with two of her.

Granny had a surprise that day because my cousins, my little brother and sisters. Aunts and Uncles came over for dinner that night. We had a beautiful night. We laughed and played like we never did before. It was great to see my sisters and brother, there are ten of us. Everything was fine until we started bussing on each other. Somebody said something about my brother and sister that really heart my heart. They called him dirty and my little sister pissy. I was embarrassed.

Being their older sibling, I stood up for them and said leave them alone. From that moment I had made a vow that I would take care of my sisters and brother. The night ended and everyone was leaving. I noticed my sisters and brother stayed behind. We all cleaned up together.

I asked my Granny were they staying the night.

Granny said, "Yes, they are going to stay here for awhile."

So we have to make room for them. Granny put Rachel, Denay and Leroy in the room with me. Chuck, Quah and Sherry will sleep in the room with Tina. Tina was not happy at all about it.

"I don't want any of them in the room with me." she said.

That made Granny mad. She snapped and called her selfish and ungrateful. I told Granny that they could just sleep in the room with me, and we did. It was only one bed, but we took the top mattress off and used them both like beds. Some of us still slept on the floor. I was not happy, but what are we going to do? Before we went to sleep we said our prayers and talked about our mother until she fell asleep. I couldn't sleep. It felt like I was up all night. I had so much running through my head. Like how could a mother leave all of her children? What did we do to deserve this? Now I have to share my room with all of them. There goes my fun. I love my brothers and sisters. None of us had our fathers in our lives. I began to cry. Why Lord did she leave us in the house dirty, with no food for days? If she didn't want us why keep having us? Her children are beautiful. Before I could finish my thoughts I heard a loud banging sound.

The sound got louder and louder, I jumped up from the floor and grabbed my little sister because she was shaking. My Uncle B-Cool went to see what the noise was. It was my mother Cindy at the door.

"Where the fuck is my kids?" she yelled.

"Come on Cindy, its three o'clock in the morning. The kids are sleep. " he said.

"B**ch, you better move and get the f*ck out of my face and go get all my kids." she said.

"I'm not going to be too many more b**ches, ok." he said staring her straight in the face.

By the time Granny got to the top of the stairs we were all crying because she keeps coming back. I'm not going to lie. We were all scared of her.

"Get ya'll shit and let's go" she said.

"Don't touch anything" my uncle yelled.

My mom is in his face and he's in hers. The kids are yelling and Granny is yelling both of them, trying to make someone listen. When suddenly out of nowhere Cindy hits my uncle. The smell of liquor fills the room. Granny tries to break it up and gets hit by mistake. Everyone paused for a little while when that happened to Granny. I didn't know what to do. I wanted to kill Cindy myself. Then there's a knock at the door. It's the cops knocking on the door with their night sticks. I went and open the door.

"Did someone call the cops?" he asked.

"I don't think so." I said.

Then Tina comes up from behind me and says "I did."

"My mom keeps coming over here bothering us and she is drunk." she said.

The officer came in by now they know

Her by name, come on Cindy, let's go, come back when your sober the cop said as he grabbed her arm firmly and led her to the door, if she comes back, call us and she's going to jail. Have a good day the officer said as he walked out.

Granny turned around and yelled at my uncle with tears in her eyes.

"Tommy, no one told you to get in it."

"Mom, I can't just sit there and watch her treat you like this."

"I can't take this anymore," granny said. "Y'all are killing me."

"Grandma don't cry," I said. "It's going to be alright."

I hate to see my grandma cry. From now on my mission is to keep a smile on her face. I can see the pain on her face. The hurt she felt watching her daughter being escorted out of the house by the police. I know exactly how she feels because that lady is my mother. I prayed and promised god that I'm was going to try and make a change in my life. I decided to return back to church. I rededicated my life to the lord that night before falling asleep. I promised myself that I was never going to sleep with the boys around the way again. I'm going to respect myself from now on. I have to help my grandmom help us. I must have cried myself to sleep because I don't remember saying amen.

It's a new day and all is well. Without my granny even asking me, I did my little sisters hair. It's crazy because even though we came from the same mom, our hair texture was different. Den ay hair was thick and curly. I did her hair first. I braided her hair with 2 big parts. She's tender headed, but yet tough with a lot of attitude. Rachel has thin curly hair. For some reason her hair would fall out in the middle, so I had to braid her hair towards the middle of her head to cover her bald spot. She's shy, but sneaky with a mean streak. Quay was the last head I did because her hair was the longest. She had the prettiest and softest of all. I braided her hair down on both sides with a part in the middle. Each braid was followed by a zigzag part. Granny washed their clothes and hung them out to dry after finished their hair, ironed their clothes and they all looked and smelled good. My brothers got their hair washed and brushed by Sherry. Sherry is older than me but younger than Teeter. Her hair steal thick with more of a tight curl. I love and respect her so much. She doesn't play though. She can kick my ass. She tells tee-tee what to do and she's younger than her, tee-tee never really had to live with us. I guess that's why she doesn't help out as much with the kids. We all ate and granny let us go outside for a while.

It's now a year later, my neighbors are helping my grandma out a lot. Some donate their children's old clothes or a friend's children clothes. Whenever a neighbor gave us something ,they would give us free toys for Christmas and free food for Thanksgiving. We would get toys and free dinner, we would be so happy. My neighbors even gave me my first job. Running back and forth to the store for them. The best part about going to the store for them was getting to know each and every one of their stories and their outlook on life.

We had this one neighbor who was blind. Her name was Ms. Jasmine. She would only send her granddaughter or me to the store. The crazy thing is she knew exactly how much money she gave you. She never seen my face, yet she knew exactly who I was. She knew my scent, my shape and my voice. I was also amazed at how clean her house was.

I love older. People and they knew they could count on me. They would always say, "If you ever need help, ask Katrina, she'd help you." Our neighbors had the permission to chastise each other's children. God forbid if they had to take you home, you might as well, kiss your ass goodbye. Whenever there was a shootout on the block, we all ran into the closest house to us. The parents would always give a quick head check making sure their children was safe. The parents would call the parents of the kids that didn't live with them to let them know that they were safe.

My grandmom would always say she had four eyes, she really meant it. Whenever she went to work, the neighbors would keep an eye on us. Back in the day your neighbors eyes was parents eyes.

I'm a mature teenage now. I know how to make money. I do hair at least once a day. My new hustle is hair braiding. My grandma don't mind as long as I clean up after myself. Plus, this is keeping me out of her pocket. She's good and I'm good.

In the projects, word gets around fast. My pockets are getting fat. I'm buying my own clothes and sneakers. I even give my granny a little something for her pocket. My clientele is growing rapidly. Every day afterschool I am doing someone's hair. I have been so busy that I don't spend a lot of time with my friends anymore. I decided to stay in the house during the week and Friday nights I'll just kick it with my homies.

I feel so damn sexy now. I don't know if it's because I have a nice shape, my tits are extra perky, stomach flat and I have a nice little rump shaker.

I think it's time to buy myself a big pair of earrings with my name in them with a matching chain and name ring. I'm not going to tell no one. I'll just surprise my haters.

I've been fighting more and more, but the sad part is, most of the time it's because of someone else problems. Anyway I got to ride for my friends. My sisters and brothers are fine. Cindy hasn't been bothering us lately. I've learned to count everyday as a blessing. I haven't been to church in a year and I don't think I'm going back. I think God is mad at me sometimes because of the way our parents treat us. And besides I'm making too much money to be going to church right now. My radar is up and I'm in the mode for a dude tonight.

It's 7p.m. and it's feeling like a nice fall night. I peek out the window to get a glance of how everyone is dressed. I inhale the cool fresh air, I love that smell. I shut the window and headed straight to my closet looking for my tightest pair of Coca-Cola jeans and my Coca-Cola shirt. I pulled out my white on white shell top Adidas. I'm feeling so good. I turned the music up and danced and sang the whole time I was doing my hair; I put a slight bump in my hair then wrapped it so that I could take a bath. I ran into Uncle Tommy on my way to the bathroom. Where are you going face? I'm about to take a bath I said in a soft tone. Hoping he wouldn't ask me to do anything for him. Alright just don't stay out past your curfew he said with a stern voice. Damn that was close. I was about to shit bricks. I laughed as I touched the door know. Damn uncle stink. I quickly turned the faucet on and poured a capful of bubble bath in the tub. I grabbed the air freshener and sprayed the air as I walked backwards gasping for fresh air, that dude smells like he haven't shit in days. I stood in grannies doorway talking to her until | felt like the coast was clear,

Oh, the water felt so very good as I slipped down in the bubbles. My mind was going at a rapid pace. All I could think about was hitting the streets. I'll meet up with Ashley and them later, I gave myself a quick but careful wash down, brushed my teeth and was out. "Bear," grandma called.

"Yes."

"Don't forget to clean the tub."

"I already did," I said.

I got dressed so fast, trying to get out before the sun went down. I wanted everyone to see me looking good. I gave granny a kiss on the cheek and promised to be in before curfew.

Damn it's crowded on the strip. That's what we call O5 building or should I say, underneath the building. All the homies are out. While waiting for Nikki to come out notice this dude I haven't seen around the way before. It was something about his smile. He had that kind of smile that made you smile even though you didn't know what the hell you were smiling for, I watched him walk down the tramp towards me. Our eyes met for the first time. Instantly, I felt a connection. All | could say was damn. I hope to see you again. I gave my lips a gentle lick with the tip of my tongue. Oh shit! I would love to have that fine ass nigga all to myself and all over my body.

"Nikki." I already knew it was you. I grabbed her hands and moved them with a little aggression. Dag girl! Nikki said. Said, why you acting like that I didn't mean it, I was trying to see which way that guy was going. What guy. The guy over there with the wavy hair and big butt, I said. Girl he comes around here all the time. They are on the fourth floor. The apartment he is in is having a "Dollar Holla" tonight.

We walked and talked until we met up with Ashley, kia, Lori, and Yvette.

"What up b**ches?" Nikki asked. She has a nasty mouth. I don't play that bitch shit. I don't say it to them so they don't say it to me.

"Who got money on the weed?" Ashley asked.

"Who got in on the forties?"

"We all do!" We answered. This is going to be a fun night. We were able to get two dime bags and three forties.

"Who house are we going over this time? No one answered.

"Well I guess we're going to the rent office," kia said.

"When we got to the rent office I tell them either. kia or Ashley are going to roll the weed because the rest of y'all hoes can't roll!"

We laughed, drank and smoked until we couldn't smoke no more. By 9:00 Pm the party was beginning. We never liked to get there too early so we would bust on each other and tell more jokes until someone got mad.

The music is bumping and I'm ready to jam. We walk back to 0-5 building and get on the elevator to go up to the fourth floor. When the elevator opened up all you could see were wall to wall people. Shit if you didn't have money to get in you could just party outside in the hall. We're all high so we decide that no one gets left behind.

All of a sudden I feel this hand squeeze my butt. I turn and it's Chub. I gave him a look that said stop playing with me. We all paid our dollar and it was on. The crowd was jumping and my crew was blended right in. Mia felt like rapping, so she asked me to hit a beat. It might sound crazy, but I liked to do everything guys liked.

We always had to steal the show. If you wanted to battle us in rapping or dancing, we did it. I got so overwhelmed that I had to throw up. I hurried over to the bathroom just in time. I washed my hands and rinsed my mouth out. Before I could wipe my mouth, he's standing in front of me. I forgot to lock the door.

"I'm sorry," he said.

"It's alright."

"You shouldn't drink if you can't handle it," he said.

"I can," I responded.

"Drinking like that doesn't make you a lady," was the last thing he said as he grabbed my hands with a gentle touch.

It's something different about him. He's a real dude. I made my way back to the girls, but this time I'm on some fall back stuff because this guy is on my mind something bad. The music slowed down and he asked me to dance. I played it off a little, acting as if I was unsure. He did exactly what I wanted him to do, take over. He whispered come on. I grabbed his hand as he led me on the dance floor. He held me by my waist, not on my butt. He danced like a man, not a dog. He whispered in my ear, "What's your name?" I felt his manhood rise, but he had total control of himself. Not one time did his hands roam where they weren't supposed to touch. I could tell he was totally into me. I whispered my name in his ear. Then I whispered "Why me?" and he responded "Why not you?" I'm straight to the point so I asked him was he seeing anyone in the O-5 building.

"That's my bull girls crib. Are you seeing anyone?"

"No," I responded.

This party ended too soon. The lights came on and someone yelled, "you don't have to go home, but you got to get the hell out of here!" We exchanged numbers and agreed to call each other tomorrow. My friends and I left the party and went straight to "Lucky Garden" to get some wings and fries. Their fries are the best. I don't know if I had the munchies or I'm just greedy. I can see my backyard from where I'm standing outside the store. I hope no one puts the chain on the door.

We grabbed our bags and went our separate ways. It's five minutes till two, I'm on time, the chain is not on and it's quite as a mouse. Every time I walk up the steps in the dark, it feels like someone's behind me. I ran up the last couple of steps. I was trying not to wake my sibling up so I took off my clothes outside of my bedroom door and hung them over the banister. I slid under the covers, closed my eyes and said my prayers and thought about how lucky I am.

The phone is driving me crazy this morning. It's a Sunday and all is well 'cause Granny is up early preparing her Sunday dinner.

"Bear," grandmom yelled. "Get the phone!" I answered it.

"Yo, Joe got killed last night," Ashley said. "The guy who lives a couple of housed down shot him." I couldn't believe what I just heard. My mouth fell to the floor. I was at a loss for words.

"Hello," Ashley said.

"I'm here," I said.

"I thought you hung up. It happened after the party right in my backyard. Are you coming out? Everyone's sitting outside around the pole across the street from Pratt."

"Yeah, I'll be out," I said and ended our conversation.

This is a very funny, but touchy moment for me. I'm feeling sad because this guy is supposed to be my cousin's baby daddy. I feel sorry for my little cousin because he'll never meet his dad. On the other hand I'm kind of glad because he was very disrespectful to the human race. I learned how to bust on people because he would bust on me all the time. I began to feel for his mother and brothers. My heart began to weep. Those were tears for his mom who had to be told that her child was dead. She couldn't believe it when she heard it. She has to clear her ears just to make sure she heard what the person was saying. Then she grabbed her heart and fell to her knees, while flashes of her son's life passed through her head, knowing that she would never be able to see her child again.

I'm thinking all of this as I rush down the long silent street, taking quick glances at everyone's face not knowing what to say. I nod my head. Without saying a word I reached the spot where he last stood.

One thing about living in the hood is if you loved someone and cried, it was alright because everyone understood. We consoled each other, some with stains of dried tears that had fallen on their faces. A tissue box was passed down the row of people. People gave whatever money they had to help the family.

It was so busy outside that I didn't even see Ashley that day. I paid my respects right then and there because I knew my heart couldn't bare going to his funeral. I didn't realize how many people truly loved Joe. This was the very first time I had experienced the loss of a close friend and I couldn't take it. I said my goodbyes and headed back home. When I got home I sat down and told grandma what happened. We sat in silence. My grandma sits at her window facing Diamond street everyday so she knew exactly who I was talking about. I can' believe it.

"He's just a boy," she says. "These children today don't cherish life anymore. I'm really scared for y'all future. My heart goes out to his mother."

As she was talking, I finally just broke down and cried in front of her, I never cry in front of anyone.

"That's why I don't like you going to those dollar parties. Someone is always starting a fight before the party is even halfway over. I can't seem to keep you out of them, so I pray to God that He keeps you and your friends in perfect peace."

I'm listening, but not listening. I love my grandmom, but sometimes she takes things too far, I thought to myself.

The phone rang and I excused myself so that I could go answer it.

"Hello," I said in a real soft voice.

"Hi, may I speak to Katrina please?"

"Hi, this is she, who's calling?"

"Devin," he replied.

My heart began to beat really fast.

"How are you doing?"

"I'm fine," I replied. "I just got some bad news."

"I hope everything is ok," he said.

"Thanks, I'll be fine, but enough about me, when can I see you?"

"You're real straight forward" he asked.

His voice is so soft and calm; it's driving me crazy. While he's talking I'm visioning his nice fluffy lips on top of mine.

"Trina!, Trina! Did you hear me?"

"What did you say?"

"I asked for your address."

"22** W. Edgley Street," I answered.

"Ok, I'll be there in a half hour."

"I'll see you when you get here."

After hanging up the phone I realized that i didn't ask my grandma could I have company. I ran upstairs to her room.

"Grandma, could I have company for a little while, please?"

"What time is it?" she asked.

"It's ten o'clock. Can I please?" She could never tell me no.

"Y'all can sit in front of the house on the steps, but not in the house. It's too late."

"Ok mommy." That's what I started calling grandma. I brushed my teeth to freshen my breath. I made sure my hair was in place and that I looked and smelled oh so fresh. I couldn't keep still. I kept looking out the window wondering which way he would come. It seemed as if time had stood still. I started wiping the table off even thought it was already clean. I dimmed the lights in the living room and turned the light off that led to the front door. I heard a soft tap on the door. I knew who it was, so I quickly opened the door. I could tell he was just as happy as I was. I couldn't believe he was standing in front of me. We gave each other a huge hug. His gentle touch and soft voice overwhelms me. He's not only fine but he can hold a great conversation. I glanced at him from head to toe with excitement bubbling inside of me at the thought of him becoming my new boyfriend.

We talked about so many things for about two hours. Laughing at the things we had in common. He's not only fine, but he's so smart. He's a student at George Washington High School. That was a plus because he's still in school in the eleventh grade. Most Black young males drop out in the eighth or ninth grade. That fact that he's working made him even more appealing to me. He didn't try to touch me in an inappropriate way. He grabs my hand every now and then with a gently touch. This is weird to me, usually the guys are feeling me up. He's not trying anything, just talking to me and looking me straight in my eyes. Every time he looks me in my eyes I put my head down and he gently lifts it back up.

Uncle Tommy comes down to the door and says with a stern voice, "It's time to say goodnight to you company young lady."

I say, "Ok."

Before leaving he says, "Hi young man, what's your name?" followed by a handshake.

"Devin," he replied.

"Nice to meet you," Uncle says as he goes back in the house. We turned to each other, gave a gentle kiss on the lips and a hug as we said our goodbyes.

"I'll call you tomorrow he said as he walked away. I quickly ran in the house and watched him walk down the street till he was no longer in my eyesight. I checked to make sure all the lights were off and made sure the front and back door was locked. Then I ran up the stairs. I don't know why I would always run up the stairs, but I just did. I always felt like someone was behind me when the lights were out. As I made it to the top of the stairs, I laughed at myself thinking how crazy I was for being so silly. I said my goodnights to granny and uncle and went in the room with my sisters and brothers. They were already sleep so I said my prayers and eventually fell asleep.

It's Monday already! I didn't realize that Sunday had come and gone. My siblings and I are up and ready for school. I do my regular routine. I get my carfare and lunch money and give granny a kiss and wait for Ashley to knock on the door. She's here. Instead of catching the bus we walked to school so that we could save our money for Friday when we party. We're having a ball talking about everything that happened over the weekend. We stopped at the store to pick up some breakfast and continued on our journey. "What's up Shorty?" Some guy yelled from across the street as we walked past the fire station. I told Ashley that he wanted her because I was already spoken for. We both laughed and kept walking without looking back. The guy yelled out, "forget y'all chicken head girls." Ashley is bad, she don't let anything slide.

"It takes one to know one," she yells back. We both gave each other a high five and continued on our way to school.

"Guess what Ashley?"

"What girl?

"Remember that guy at the party I danced with last weekend?"

"No girl, who don't you dance with," she said.

"Don't be smart, but you right."

Just as I was about to tell her we started walking through the front door of the school. An outsider approached us ,so we ended the conversation. We said our goodbyes and off we went. I'm in advisory class and it's about fifteen students in the class. We usually take roll and study for a while, but this day was too good to be true, until this boy started busting on people. I didn't feel like it today. Why is it that the dirty boys are always the ones that do all the busting?

"Stop playing Bernard!" I said.

"You think you cute with your big ass nose," he said along with some other things that made me even madder, I couldn't take it anymore. I began yelling, "you're always trying to talk about somebody with your dirty ass self!"

"Look at you with your nappy head and dirty jeans. I'm going to say what the rest of them are thinking but won't say to you."

The class went silent. You could hear a pin drop. That same teacher that sat there the whole time sleeping while we're in her class, opened up her eyes with a slight lift of her eyebrow, then and gave me a look like I know that's not you. But it was too late. The class began to laugh extra loud. I felt kind of good at that moment. I made him extra mad. Before I knew it, he done kicked the back of my chair so hard that I jerked forward. I jumped up in his face and it was on. The class started yelling and we fought for a couple minutes, but it seemed like a hour. That woke Ms. Turner up, but she couldn't move fast enough. We made it to the hall. Other classes started coming out into the hall. I was like a cat on a dog. I ripped off his shirt, and scratched up his face. He got some good hits in, but all of a sudden I felt someone tugging at my arm. That was it I'm in trouble now, I thought as we walked down that long hall to the dean's office. I was already in trouble, so I rolled my eyes at him and cracked my knuckles to let him know that it wasn't over. We made it to the dean's office and I was suspended. They called my house and sent me home early with a pink slip. We couldn't leave at the same time so they sent Bernard home first. I was given my slip and escorted to the front door. On the way home I thought to myself, how upset my granny was going to be. I hated to disappoint her, but he had it coming.

Chapter 6

THE EVIL LADY IS HERE!

"Why the hell is you not in school?"

Why the hell is you here is what I really wanted to ask her? But I didn't because I wanted to live. I answered her question real slow with a low shaky voice, "I was suspended for three days."

"I didn't hear your dumbass!" she said as if she's so smart after having all these damn kids at such a young age. She's got a nerve, I thought to myself.

"Girl I asked you a question?

"I said got suspended for three days for fighting."

"Get dressed and go to the store for me," she said. I slipped on a pair of sweat pants and a t-shirt and ran to the store feeling like I got off easy this time. Mommy didn't put me on punishment and the evil lady, "Cindy," didn't do anything either. I'm a good I thought.

"Can I have a Pepsi, a pack of Newport 100's and two packs of Now-n-Laters?"

I was in and out. The store was empty because everyone was in school. As I'm walking out the door, I walked right into the police.

"Come here young lady. Why aren't you in school?"

"I got suspended," I answered.

"Then you should be in the house," he said. "Where do you live?"

I pointed across the street to show him. Then he told me to get in the car. I noticed Cindy looking out the window at me. She opened the door and yelled, that's my daughter, I sent her to the store.

"I'm going to let you go this time, but the next time I'm taking you in for truancy," he said. I walked across the street and jumped over the fence that led to our back door, I placed my hand on the knob and gave it a slight turn, not knowing that Cindy was opening the door too, I fell into the house. Then out of nowhere Cindy starts to swing on me with the extension cord from the washing machine. The bag from the store fell to the floor. I was trying to block and cover myself. It hurts so bad, it feels like my skin is peeling from my body.

"You trying to hit me back? I'll kill you little girl. You think it's ok to keep getting suspended?" We were knocking things over, screaming and yelling until my grandmother came down stairs to make her stop.

"Cindy! Stop hitting that girl like that. You're not even supposed to be here! Get your stuff and leave."

"That's their problem," the evil lady said. Every time I chastise them y'all always in my business. Stop telling me what the fu*k to do with my kids!"

"If you don't leave, I'm calling the police," granny said. "Look at her she's bleeding.

"I don't give a f*ck," she said while gathering her things. I'm standing there in a state of shock with tears in my eyes, rubbing my wounds. I couldn't believe what just happened. The house was a mess. The chairs were knocked over, the lamp had fallen to the floor, the Pepsi bust all over the floor, her cigarettes were wet and the stereo was pulled out from the wall, that's where she got the extension cord from. My grandmother tapped me on the shoulder to get my attention, go upstairs and clean up while I clean this mess up. "Ok," I said as I went up the steps. While I was in the bathroom I notice the evil lady was walking down the block still talking trash to my grandmom. I quickly moved away from the window so that she couldn't see me. The thought of me getting away with being suspended, I knew it was too good to be true. I went back downstairs to help granny clean up the mess. I couldn't help but ask granny why Cindy keeps coming around.

"I don't know baby, but we have to keep her in our prayers."

I've been avoiding Devin for about two weeks. He finally reached me by phone.

"Hello, can I please speak to Katrina."

"This is she," I said.

"What's ups Trina? How have you been? I've been calling you almost every day!

This little boy kept answering the phone. Did he give you my messages?"

"No," I said pretending not to know he called.

"Well anyway, now that I have you on the phone, when do you think I could see you again?" My scars are almost gone, I reminded myself.

"Maybe Saturday," I responded. We talked for a little while longer and then hung up. I'm standing in the hallway downstairs next to the front door thinking to myself why do my siblings and I have to have such a horrible life. The tears started rolling down my face. There was a knock on the door, I quickly wiped my face with the sleeve of my shirt and asked, "Who is it?"

"Ashley," she said. I opened the door and it was Lori, Yvette, kia, Nikki and Tiny.

"What's up girl? Are you coming out? We are about to go to Rec Center to the basketball game." I fixed my hair into a ponytail with a bang in the front. I put on my big earrings and leather jacket and we were out.

As we were walking down the street past the building, Tiny yells out, "Guess what b**ches?" Then she pulls out three blunts already rolled up and we began smoking. We passed the blunt back and forth as we walked and we started singing pass the "Duchy to the left." We all started laughing 'cause we are high. Yvette plays to much 'cause when she high she starts busting on people or starts playing the game "open neck no respect." We are almost there so she calms down a little. All the guys around the way are walking in their own little groups. They were looking real fly, but I made it a point not to mess with too many of the guys in the neighborhood. We went up the stairs that led to the gym. It's wall-to-wall niggas in here. It smells like sweaty balls mixed with chlorine in here. We all laughed and went to find a spot where we could sit together, the game had already started. The score was ten to zero. Rec center is winning. The music is jumping and we are talking shit to each other. I'm a little laid back because I have a lot on my mind and smoking weed doesn't make it any better. Sometimes I think too much. Tired now I just want to feel good. I'm high and I don't want to waste it on unwanted energy. My girls started dancing and dropping it like it was hot bringing attention to us. There was a group of guys we didn't know on the sideline looking real good. They looked like a pack of starburst, all different flavors. I stared in their direction and took notice to one of the guys was Devin. He didn't notice me so I continued to stare just to see what he was like while out with the boys. I whispered to Ashley, "Remember that guy I was telling you about? That's him over there. He's the short light brown skinned one with the wavy hair, slanted eyes, thin mustache, thick lips and big butt. Sike!" I said laughing. "He's the one with the white and blue Coca-Cola sweater and light blue stone wash jeans."

"Girl he's fine," she said.

"I know right."

We continued to watch the game and he made his way over to me. He placed his hand on my waist and whispered, "What's up? I didn't know you were going to be here."

His voice is soft. It makes me want to melt.

"Come here," he says as he grabbed my hands. I don't know if it's 'cause I'm high, but he looks extra good to me. We walk away from the crowd but not too far enough that my friends were out of eyesight. The more we talked the closer he got and I let him. He turned me around so that my back was facing his . He gently places my butt on his penis kissing the side of my neck and it feels soo good.

"Stop! They're looking at us."

"So what, aren't you my girl? Well, let them look."

In a way I'm feeling this because he's my man and now everyone knows it.

After the game ended he told his boys that he would catch up with them later. He shook their hands letting them know that he was ok. When my girls finally decided to come and get me, I told them that I was going with Devin. I introduced him to them. Their reaction was totally different. kia was out spoken, she'll say whatever she feels.

"How are you going to just leave us like that?

"Because I'm taking her with me," Devin respond.

"Al'right who he think he's talking to?"

I quickly intervened and said, "I'll see y'all later." Giving them a look as if to say don't do it y'all, I really like him.

"Bye freak, "kia said as they turned and walked away.

"Whatever hater." We stood there for a while talking as we

watched everyone leave the center. The janitor Mr. Duke came out and locked the doors. Good night young people he said as he walked down the steps.

"I'll walk you home," Devin said after giving me a kiss with his tongue almost reaching the back of my throat. I don't know what it is about him, but I really like him. He makes me feel so safe when I'm with him, he's a man of his word. He walked me all the way to my front door and gave me a hug before we said our goodbyes. I think I'm falling in love with him, but he'll never know. I turned the door knob and made my way pass the same area I had not too long ago stood with my eyes filled with tears. How can a girl like me be so lucky? Out of all my friends, why did he pick me? Whatever the reason is I'm happy.

Everyone is up early today. My uncle is off to work. My little brother and sister is up and dressed for school. I went into granny's room to get my lunch money and to say goodbye.

"Mommy," I said. She didn't answer me. I tapped her on the shoulder to make sure she wasn't sleep. It was strange 'cause grandmom was always the first one up making sure we were up and dressed for school.

"Mommy, do you hear me?" I continued to tap her on the arm. She's staring me right in the face but she's not answering. Tears began to run down her face.

"What's wrong Mommy? Are you in pain? Can you talk?" She couldn't answer me. I began to cry.

"Please Mommy, you're scaring me. Do you want me to call the police?

She gave me a look that I'll never forget. It looked as if she was saying please help me. I called 911 and while I waited for the cops to come I got my siblings together and sent them off to school. I didn't want them to see our grandmom like that. After they left I began crying. The police knocked on the door. I opened the door and told them that she was upstairs in the backroom to the left. A couple of minutes later the fire department came. I explained to them what happened and they told me that she's having a stroke. They placed her on the stretcher and carried her down the steps to the ambulance. I kissed her on the cheek and told her that I would let everyone know what happened and I reassured her that I would take care of the kids while she was gone. I stood there and watched while they put her in the ambulance and strapped her down. The guy waved his hand to signal the driver to pull off. I stood there for a moment and watched them disappear out of sight. I was still in disbelief. I walked back to the house. Everyone was outside standing on their steps watching.

"Don't cry Trina, she'll be alright baby, Ms. Edna said. I couldn't respond. It felt like my whole world was crashing all around me. The very air that I was breathing had left my body. What am I going to do? How am I going to tell my family that mommy was sick? I wiped my face as I approached my front door. I tried to pull myself together before I made the first phone call.

"Hello Aunt Linda?"

"Yes, who's this? Is this Trina?"

"Yes," I said.

"Why are you home and why are you crying? She asked with a stern but scared voice.

"Mommy was just rushed to the hospital," I said.

"What happened?"

"She was having a stroke."

"Tell me what hospital she's at so that Tammy and I can go see her."

"She's going to Temple Hospital," I said.

"Stay by the phone just in case I need to know what meds she take. I'll let you know how she is doing when I get there."

"Ok," I said as we hung up. I felt a little better after talking to Aunt Linda because I knew that she would call everyone to let them know what happened. That relieved some stress off of me.

I'm upstairs sitting in grandmom's rocking chair praying to God, whom I haven't had much to say to lately, asking Him to please have mercy on my granny. She's a nice lady who loves all her grandchildren and we need her lord, Amen. I got up and started cleaning up her room. I made her bed, wiped off the dressers, swept and mopped her bedroom floor. I didn't want granny to do anything when she came home so I decided to clean the whole house. Then I took some chicken out for dinner.

Later that day, instead of it being just my siblings and I at the house, all of my cousins came over to the house because their parents were at the hospital with granny. All of grannies children were at the hospital except my mom. The house was packed. Kids were running around everywhere. I refused to let them in grandmom's room because it needed to stay clean for her.

The phone rang and it was Aunt Linda.

"Trina?"

"Yes," I answered.

"Did my kids and Aunt Tammy's kids get there yet?"

"Yes," I said.

"Well keep your eyes on them until we get there. Mommy's not coming home tonight. They said she is paralyzed on her left side. We'll be home shortly." When I hung up the phone everything hit me and I cried out like a baby. I couldn't keep it together.

"Why are you crying?" They kept asking, so I sat everyone down and told them what was going on. Now everyone was crying and the house was a mess.

"Stop crying and let's clean up before they come home," said. To my surprise they listened. Uncle Tommy got home first. I don't think he's in a good mood 'cause he was yelling at us for everything we did.

"Shut the hell up," he yelled. We were kids and no one was listening. Don't make me come down there he said in his Marine voice. Yes we all said together like we were in a choir.

We were so bored. We were just sitting around looking at each other in the face. My sister decided to start busting on my brother. Whoever laughed the loudest was next in line to get "bust" on. We started having so much fun and then all of a sudden we heard a loud sound. Everyone got quiet; you could hear a pin drop. It was glass all over the floor. Then Uncle Tommy came downstairs and asked, "Who in the hell did this?" We were so scared that nobody answered.

"Alright, everyone is going to get it, go get George!" He yelled.

That's the name he gave his belt. He lined all of us in size order; smallest to the biggest. If you're wondering if I got beat too, yes I did!

"Drop them!" He said telling us to pull down our pants. He wanted to hit flesh only. Some called out for their moms, while others yelled out for grandmom, waiting for her to come to the rescue. They forgot she was in the hospital and there was no chance of her hearing them. We all sat on the couch crying and rubbing our wounds. This time nobody said a word. We all sat and watched as Uncle cleaned up the broken lamp. Deep down inside I wanted to tell him to keep his mother fucking hands off of me before I smack his ass back and that it wasn't me. I knew better than that though. It was weird 'cause it felt like he heard me. He looked at me and said, "Get your eyeballs of me young lady!" Not much longer after that my aunts came in. Their eyes were so puffy. I've never seen them so sad. They went straight upstairs to grandmom's room to have a meeting. A little while later, Uncle Jim came over and they started the meeting. They shut grandma's door so that we couldn't hear anything. When they finally came out all they said was get y'all coats and then they left. We knew nothing. We ate dinner and got ready for bed. As I lay on my bed I couldn't believe that granny didn't come home. Things will never be the same from this day on.

It's been two years since grandmom's stroke. She lost most of her functioning on her left side and she need help to get washed and dressed. You never know how God works and how He does things, but thank you Lord for saving my grandmom. Everyday it's the routine; I'd wash and iron grandma's clothes for the whole week, cook dinner and clean the whole house. We don't go to church any more 'cause granny could barely walk. I don't think she likes people feeling sorry and staring, so the deacons at the church will come over and give her holy communion.

Monday through Friday when I have to go to school my aunts would come over to get her dressed and make her breakfast. I would take over afterschool. I love my grandmom and there wasn't anything that I wouldn't do for her, I haven't been kicking it with my friends as much, but it's ok. Some Friday's after I cooked, cleaned and got mommy dressed and in bed, she would let me go out to the "Dolla Holla" parties as long as I made it in before curfew. I always placed her potty next to her bed just in case she had to go in the middle of the night. We came up with a way for her to get on it without walking or falling. All she had to do was to sit-up in the bed and slide to the right, then lift herself onto the chair. She would do the same getting back into the bed. I always placed a pitcher of ice water and her meds, separated for the whole week for day and night, on her night table with a cup of water just in case she got thirsty.

Granny taught me how to pay all of her bills. She sat right there and helped me count the money out for each bill. She gave me the authority to sign her checks and to use her credit cards after she contacted the proper people to put me down as a second user on her cards. Grandmom always said your credit is how you get stuff, so take care of it. Taking care of granny is a hard job to do, but each and every day that passes it gets easier and easier, she's so worth it. I love to see that sparkle in her eyes. It lets me know that I'm doing an okay job. Every day she wakes up I feel so blessed.

My siblings are getting big and can pretty much take care of themselves, somewhat. My oldest sister, oh well, it's not much I can say about her, she stays out of my way and I do the same. Uncle Tommy has been acting more like the punisher, just waiting on the side line for someone to mess up so he can pull George out. Just saying that name scares me. It's like saying Ike and Tina. I'm so funny sometimes. If you didn't get it, just laugh anyway, LOL. But on a more serious note, Cindy stops pass every now and then. When she does it's never on good terms. She steals our food, clothes and to remind grandmom how she stole her kids from her.

"These are my kids," she'd say while stumbling to the side with the smell of liquor on her breath.

"I'll take these mother fuckers if I want. No one can tell me what to do," she said. She never once turned to granny to say thank you mom for helping take care of my kids. I truly believe that she was the cause of grandmom getting sick. She doesn't make things any better showing up acting like this. Never mind that her mother couldn't get around like she used to. That just made it that much easier for her to do whatever she wanted until Uncle Tommy got mad enough and knocked her on her behind. It seemed as if she got used to that to. It didn't faze her at all. She just kept coming back for more. That's why I was so afraid of her. I kept telling myself that one of these days I was going to fight her back. Imagine that! God forbid.

I try to stay home more. If we have to practice our dance for a show we would meet at my house and practice in the living room.

If we wanted to get high, I would try my best to stay away from granny until I came down off my high and spray myself with perfume. Most of the time, we would take a walk around the block to smoke. We thought we were so slick. When we wanted to have a drink, we would pay one of the drunks on the corner to get us a bottle. We would mix it with juice so no one knew we were drinking. My favorite drunk name was Slick. He would always say why buy it at the store when you can get it at the door, my friends and I would laugh so hard. We would grab our bottle and head back into the house. Uncle Tommy would be so high himself that he never noticed. We just pretended that the bottles in the trash were his. We like the same things he liked. It only worked on the weekends though. Monday through Thursday you could forget it. He had to be up too early in the morning so he didn't get high during the week. I pretty much had his schedule down pack. I knew what time he went to bed and what time he woke up. I was good right? So, at night I would call Kasheem over and he would stay with me until it was time for him to go. We spent plenty of time together, when he would come over, we'd have sex downstairs. Right under their noses and no one ever knew. I had it all planned and that was a chance that I was willing to take. Hopefully I won't get caught though.

It's almost like he lives with me. He's here every day after school. We have dinner together and he helps me with my homework and chores I don't know if it's just me, but if feels like we're married with children and our parents and long lost uncle lives with us. My siblings just love him. Granny and my aunts and uncles like him a lot. They don't even tell him it's time for him to go home anymore. When it's time for me to call it a night, we sleep together, I would pretend to walk him to the door and say goodnight. I would close the door behind him, but he would never leave. Just like clockwork after I shut the front door I would turn off the lights and motion for him to walk with me up the stairs, the same time as me until we reached the top. He would walk into my bedroom and shut the door behind him. I would walk to grandma's room to get her ready for bed. I would even sit with her for a while until I got tired. I would kiss her on the cheek and say goodnight. I would always take a shower before I went to bed because I never knew if we were going to have sex, I needed to always be ready. After my shower would tap on the door to let him know that it was me. He would open the door and that's when playing house would begin. Whatever we needed to say to each other we would whisper it. We would lay and watch television for hours until we thought everyone was asleep. Oh how we would make love, and yes I said make love. He loved me and I felt the same way. When we made love it felt like the heavens opened up. I would jump inside my skin at the very touch of him. His soft voice would calm me like a lion being tanned. He did things to me that I have never had done before. He taught me how to do things that I was too ashamed to say. I loved him and I wanted to please him. I heard once that whatever you won't do, someone else will. I wasn't going for that I would knock a b**ch out for him. When we were done he would lay behind me and wrap his arms around me and fall asleep. I would lie there trying and asking God to forgive me and hope that we would never get caught.

I need some fresh air, these walls are starting to close in on me. I have an appointment to do Ms. Pauline's hair at four o'clock today. I changed my clothes and grab my bag with all of my supplies. I'll be doing hair at her house. That's more money for me because I charge extra if I have to travel to you. There's nothing like fast money I'm thinking as I put my lip gloss on my lips. It's nice out today and the fresh air feels good as it blows through my hair, while I'm waiting for the 33 buses, my friend sees me and decides to wait with me. His name is Buss. We knew each other since we were little. He always had a soft spot in his heart for me and I knew it. We always had a on again off again type of friendship. The bus finally came and we gave each other a quick hug and said our goodbyes. I got off the bus on Girard Avenue and walked two blocks over, I rang the door bell and Ms. Pauline welcomed me in. We will be over there she said pointing to a tall bar stool that sat in front of this bar she had in the living room. I looked around the room. Her home was beautiful. Her decor was black and gold and I liked it a lot. This is what I'm talking about. Family pictures were hanging up on the wall. She grabbed a little chair and asked would I like something to drink?

"No thank you," I said.

"Well let's get started," she said as she turned the TV on. She wanted her hair braided like Cleopatra. I sectioned her hair and began to braid it. I looked down at my watch it was 5:30 pm. I should be done in 2 hours I thought to because her head is so small. The conversation was great. I learned a lot about her. She's very funny. It's always good to talk to older women who have a lot of knowledge.

"Girl you braid tight, I need to take a pain pill. Are you mad about something?" Then she started to laugh.

"No," I responded. Two more braids and I'll be done. I pulled out the oil sheen, gel and scissors. I grabbed a palm size amount of gel and rubbed it together, then, I rubbed into her hair. I cut her bang straight across and I cut the sides at a zero degree angle around the nape of her head. I sprayed oil sheen in her hair and removed the cape. She walked across the room to look in her mirror. A look of appreciation came across her face. She turned to me to show her approval of the job.

"How much she asked?"

"Thirty five," I said. She gave me forty as she thanked me and told me she would call me again. I asked her to please tell a friend. That fast money is good money. I'll buy my grandmom something nice just to let her know how much I love her.

I caught the 33 bus going north, back toward my house. Instead of going home I decided to hit the streets and have a little fun. I didn't walk on Diamond street. I took Edgely Street and walked on the back street of my block past the rent office up to the O5 building. I'll go see my cousin Nikki. I haven't seen her in a while. She's my best cousin in the whole world. No matter what she does to me I just can't seem to get enough of her. There is always someone under the building sitting on the ramp I know.

"What's up Charlie? I said as I was making my way to the elevator. The elevator is taking too long so I decided to take the stairs. The smell of urine is so bad it makes you want to puke. I knocked on the door and my cousin Gee-Gee answered.

"Hey Batman," I said. That was her nickname the family give her.

"What's up Fuzz Face," she said followed by a slap on my back. We both laughed because that's just what we do. My aunt was not home as usual. Nikki was already dressed.

"Hey Squirrel."

"Don't play bitch, she said with that nasty mouth of hers. She doesn't mean any harm, that's just how she talks.

"You want to get some weed?"

"Yeah, I'm in." I said and gave her three dollars on a bag.

I haven't heard from Devin all day, but its ok. Gina rolled up the weed and it was on. We were smart enough not to smoke in the house, so we did it in the fire escape. We got to laughing and busting on each other. Before we knew it, the party had started. The party was on the tenth floor. We went in to freshen up. We sprayed perfume on us to help take away the smell of the weed. We caught the elevator up to the tenth floor to the party and met up with the rest of the crew. Everyone was in the hallway. It felt like we were walking the red carpet. It feels so good to be loved or is it the weed making me feel this way. I have so many associates that I hang with so I decided to walk over to Missy and her crew and smoke some more weed with them.

I really like them because I don`t have to worry about getting into a fight with no one. All they do is laugh and have fun, most of the time I`m the one telling all the jokes.

We never made it into the party this night, it was to hot inside any way. The music was jumping and the weed kept being passed.

Just to my surprise who gets off the elevator? Devin, I heard him from a distance asking Nikki "where Trina at ?" She motioned for him to walk towards me. As he got closer I noticed that their wasn't a smile on his face.

When he finally reached me he held his hand out for me to grab it. I placed my hand in his making sure that he had a firm grip as he lead me through the crowd, he gave the girls a half hello. While at the squeezing my hand really hard to let me know that he was displeased with me for some reason.

Pretending everything was ok , I walked with him quietly not causing any attention. I knew if my friends knew what was going on they would have jumped him. Everything happened so fast all I remember was getting off the elevator than the next thing was being

in William Dick school yard fighting this guy that I thought was so nice and sweet. He asked me "who was the dude that I was talking to and why didn't I call him ?"and

Before I could answer his question he slapped me like I was his child. He ripped off my shirt that I had on and broke my earrings in half along with popping my chain. I couldn't believe it was happening and began to have flash backs of fighting Freddy in this very same place.

That's when I began to fight back even harder. I thought if

he beats me up at least he'll know that wasn't going to just let him beat on me. I dug my nails deep in his skin until he started to bleed, what ever high I had before I met up with him was completely gone. He was much stronger than me so eventually I gave up and began to cry." It's over I said, I don't want to be with anybody that wants to hurt me .I'm tired of fighting!

Then I guess he felt bad nd grab me, putting his

Arms around my waist saying" I'm sorry, some dude told me you was talking to your old boy friend and I got mad! Was it true?" I said" yes but we was waiting at the bus stop together ,and when the bus came we went our separate ways." Now he's trying to kiss me like nothing ever happened. He's fixing my hair and took of his shirt and gave it to me to wear since he ripped mines off. Now he telling me that he'll replace my things that he broke. I'm not going to lye, it took me a moment to get myself together before leaving the school yard. My heart is completely broken and I knew rite than and their that our l ove had changed for the worst. The real him had finally showed up and showed out. This time when we got to my house instead of letting him in, I turned around and stopped him at the front door, holding my arm out so he couldn't get past I asked him to leave. My eyes where filled with tears I shut the door and never looked back.

Chapter 7

THE TIME OF MY LIFE, PROM TIME

He's supposed to go on my prom with me, tickets where already paid for in advance. I haven't heard from Devin so I decided that I was not going to go is what I was telling the father of one of the lil girls hair that I do every two weeks. His name is James he's very nice and respectful. He calls me sugar chriss, we would often have conversations every now and than. His advise to me was ,this is the best time of your life and if you don't go on your Prom your going to regret it for the rest of your life." Don't let one monkey stop the show!" " I don't have a date, and I don't want to go by myself neither do I have a dress a car or money for my pictures, with out taking a breath I manage to say. I waited to late to pay the balance on the tickets." Not wanting to continue the conversation I try to change the subject, for some strange reason we where rite back at it again. Before I realized it I was saying yes to Mrs James taking me on my prom. First I thought he was playing a joke on me , but the look on his face let me know that he was serious. " Ask your grandmother if it's ok, if she says yes let me know how much money you need to pay for your pictures and the balance on your tickets!" I'll let my wife know that I want to take you on your prom ok? " Yes " I said I finished his daughter hair and receive my pay. As I walked out the door I had a I can't believe it look on my face ,thinking why me and how could I be so lucky. This man has money for days and he's willing to spend some on me with no strings attached. I'm so blessed , for that moment in my life I 'm not worried about how my boy friend feels.

Filled with excitement I couldn't hardly get my words out rite as I tried to explain to my grand mom what just happen. " Slow down baby I can't understand what your saying! " granny said I took a deep breath" Mommy , Mr James Mrs Ruth husband told me to ask you if it was alright if he could take me on my prom? If so he'll pay for every thing."

"I'll think about it " I couldn't wait so I said "Please" I gave her that sad look that she couldn't resist. "Alright" she said. I gave her a big hug and a kiss as I turned the corner to go to my bedroom, I ran rite into my uncle B cool girlfriend Gina. She was so happy for me that she offered to help me find my dress. I mumbled to myself that God is so good as I shut the door to my bedroom and decided to call it the night. .

Things are moving to fast two days later I'm over my soon to be aunt Gina house trying on a beautiful royal blue dress. The house is filled with people I have never met before. Her parents and siblings was so nice, her baby sister told me if I could fit her last year prom dress I could wear it. Theirs a bathroom to the right in the dinning room your more than welcome to use it to try on your dress. I grabbed the dress and proceeded to the powder size bathroom. My cloths quickly fell to the floor and I so carefully slid my size 10 into that beautiful dress in hopes that I could fit it. I couldn't reach the zipper in the back so I called Gina in the bathroom to help me. I took in a deep breath and held my stomach while she zipped me up. You look so nice she said "come on out so my family can see you" with excitement in her eyes.

I have never felt so nervous before as I walked out to show her family I looked. Everyone was so happy for me, your beautiful they yelled look at you her mom said followed by "it's yours Trina!" After getting the family approval I went back to the bathroom got dress, thanked every one and was on my way. Straight from there I went to my friend house Chevy to get my hair done. Guess what? She did it for free! Don't say that God wont make a way for you. I hurried home so I could get my money to make it to the shoe store on time to get something nice to match my dress. When I got there Gina had already picked up my shoes and fix them up to match my dress. Once I found that out the tears began to fall from my eyes. She gave me a hug and said" go take your bath and relax so you'll be ready for your make up. I never had this much attention before my bath water was ready, I took off my clothes slid in tube and let my body soak in the luke worm water. No one knew it but I thought about how I wish my boyfriend was going with me. Tears fell down my face just thinking about how I wanted my mom and dad to be their with me on such a special occasion like this. I got out the tub and washed my face and the emotions that came alone with it.

I wrapped myself in my robe, opened the door and all I could hear was my aunts & uncles talking to my grand mom. My friends and cousins are all down stairs waiting to see me leave out for my prom. Gina came in my room to help me get dress and to also put on my makeup. This is my first time wearing makeup, my grand mom gave me her pearl neckless and her earrings. As she placed the chain around my neck she kissed me on the cheek and told me how proud of ome she was. When I turned around to look at her ,her eyes was filled with tears, without saying a word I let her know how much I love her with a big hug. "Show time" I said as I walked to the top of the stairs. " She's ready" aunt P yelled out, the front door was now wide open. I slowly walked down the stairs, when my hit the bottom step, I quickly scan the room and stepped out the door. The flashes kept coming my friends

,family and neighbors start yelling look over here. The camera nearly blinded me, as I adjusted my eyes to see clearly their he was my date standing their waiting for me looking like a tall glass of chocolate that I was to young to drink. The smile he gave me when he saw me let me know that I was looking like the bomb and he was well pleased. I fill like Cinderella, I went from rags to riches. When we made it to the end off the block Mr. Jay had a Cadillac civil all white with royal blue roof top. I still can't believe this is all for me, I whispered to him as he opened the car door for me. The pictures was still snapping as he sat down and locked his seat belt. His wife leaned in and gave him a kiss goodbye, I guess that was to remind him to remind him that he had a wife waiting for him at home and not to forget it. He drove through the crowd of people as they waved goodbye to us. I'll never forget this night we dance to make it last forever by Keith Swet. Mr. J did exactly what he said he was gong to do, he paid for my pictures and $100.00 dollars. He never at one time try any thing disrespectful to me. Mr. J brought me rite back home from where he picked me up from, gave me a hug and said" Sugar Criss I really enjoyed myself and said goodnight." I'll never forget him nor the people who donated their time and talents to me on this special day. Dreams do come true I said to myself as I took my cloths off and went to bed, thanking the Lord for a beautiful day.

It's been weeks now and I haven't heard a word from Devin yet, so I've made up in my mind that I'll give this guy Bus a play. He seems to be such a nice guy and I knew him since we where lil kids. On this particular day that I decided to take his phone number and also let him know that I was a free bird. After I told him that he landed a big kiss of a life time on me. Secretly I've been wanting to know what those lips feel like. He lives in the next block from me and from my house I could see his house. We decided to meet each other at the end of the block to sit on the pole to take time out to know each other better. That's when I found out that he was real silly and likes to play a lot. This was different for me because I'm used to dating older guys who's more laid back. He's so fine that I think I can look pass all that silliness! We walked through the block holding hands until we made our way to the front door of my house.

I notice that he was wanted to give me a hug good bye so I reached over and grabbed him by his arm and gave him another kiss but this time giving him some tongue, his lips taste like what ever candy he had just eaten. So I bit down on his lip softly and released it and told him "that your not ready for this yet" and gently pushed him away. With all that kissing going on I became a lil thirsty, so I stop in the kitchen to get a glass of ice water before going up stairs. For some strange reason I didn't lock my bedroom door, so I just walked in. The light was off so I reached to the right and flipped the switch up."ooh you scared me! What you doing hear?" With fear in my voice of not knowing how much he had saw." You wouldn't return my phone calls and kept trying to avoid me ,so I decided to come see you." Your grand mom let me in" He said I'm sitting in your room because the door was opened every one else went upstairs and I think to bed. I stood their with this dumb look on my face, I couldn't talk so he kept talking. " I heard about you going on your prom without me ,how can you just do something like that?" I guess he was trying to flip the script like always. " No answer?" he said then he stood up with this blank look in his eyes and walked towards me ,I flinched when he raised his hand to place it on his chin." Is this what you do to your man?" Cheat ! This time I managed to say " No " with a scratchy voice. " So why are you out there hold-ing hands and kissing that same dude you told me you was just friends with ?" " We just start talking a couple of days ago" I said Then he said " You minds well brake up with him cause we back together!" " And please don't let me find out that you and Bus are still together, and yes I said Bus" I know his name and even played basketball with his a couple of times! He said as he pulled me close to him and gave me a forceful kiss that I didn't want. I sat down on my bed thinking to myself what am I going to do now? I don't want to start any trouble between them so I decided to give him another try. He walked over to the closet and reached in his pocket to retrieve a jewelry box, he turned around and opened it. Their was a pair of stop sigh earrings with my name and his name engraved in them. Their was another box with a rope chain with the matching dog tag to match my earrings. I was so happy that I completely forgot about every thing we had been through as he helped me put every thing on. " didn't I tell you that I'd replace every thing I broke." That night we had make up sex, it sounds crazy but that make up sex is sometimes the best sex. After wards we fell asleep with his arms wrapped around me so tight.

Just my luck Bus had to be standing in the front door when Devin and I walked out of my house. Devin tried to be smart when he saw him by placing his arms around my waist and walking with me from behind. My heart dropped because I didn't want him to find out like this, so I tried not to make eye contact with him, wondering to myself how could I hurt someone like this if I truly liked him the way I proclaimed to? From that day on I made a promise to myself to never get involved with him anymore unless it was truly over with me and Devin or any one else for that matter. To my surprise he's bolder than I thought cause I tried to avoid him so bad that I didn't realize that he was standing right in front of me, shacking hands with Devin. " Whats up man?" he said and in return Devin said the same. Making sure he looked me in my eyes, he gave me a look that said how could you with out saying a word. I just bit down on my lip and looked down to the toward the ground as if I was sorry. Lets go babe is what he said as we walked away with the proof that we was now a couple again from the looks of my new earrings and chain set that had our names engrave in them. To make matters worst my hair was pulled back in a ponytail with a side bang,I had a fresh white shirt with stone wash jeans and a pair of high top white reeboks on. I couldn't lie if I wanted to by trying to say something, the proof was in the pudding!

No I didn't walk down the else for graduation because I had to attend summer school before I could receive my diploma. I passed summer school with an A and now I have my high school diploma. My granny was so happy when I placed that Diploma in her hand, just as I promised her. I wish you could have seen her face, I was her second grand child who graduated from school. I found out that even my so called best friend was telling people that I went on my prom for nothing because she didn't graduate! What you call that I jealous, so I wanted to prove her wrong by placing my diploma in her face to rub it in and that's just what I did. That left her standing their with that dum look on her face, from then on I decided that ion I'll see her in traffic! When I closed that door I began to spend more with my boy friend and our family instead. when ever I wasn't with Devin I was out doing hair making money. The more hair I did the more I decided to go back to school to get my certification in Cosmetology.

My name is now is spreading around the PJs like water in a good way, clients are coming from the left and right. I'm doing hair every day except on Sundays. I forgot to tell yall that my boy friend cuts hair so we getting that money, and not by selling drugs but by using our talents.

When we meet up at the end of the day were so excited to see each other even the more, No more fighting it's all about us now. Every Friday I give my grand mom a couple of dollars just to let her know how much I love her even though she never want to take it from me. My siblings are getting older and can kind of fin for their selves now. I'm truly thinking about moving and getting a apartment with Devin, things are really looking up for us now.

Why don't I feel like getting out of my bed? I just want to sleep my life away. For some strange reason the food that some-one is cooking in the house smells awful. It's almost 1:00 in the after noon and everyone is up except me so I managed to pill my-self up out of the bed. I slipped on my slippers to proceed down the hall to wash my face and brush my teeth. As I made my way pass each room I noticed that no one was in them, every one was downstairs sitting at the table eating Bacon, eggs, potatoes as I got closer the smell of the eggs made me sick! " I made your plate " Tee said ,now I'm scared because first of all she don't really like me neither can she cook! Not wanting to be rude I took her up on her offer and reached out for her to hand me my plate, as soon as that plate hit my hand the smell became overwhelming. I jumped up and ran to the back door cause Lord knows I couldn't make it to the bathroom. When I turned around to get some tissue , I couldn't help but notice the look on granny face.

I sat their for a moment just looking at every one as they conversate with each other ,then starring at the Jesus picture on the wall praying on the inside, Lord please don't let me be preg-nant. That's when granny asked me with a stern voice " What's wrong with you?" " I noticed that your sleeping a lot ,not eating right , most of all your not doing hair like you used to, and that's not you." I reach out for the tissue and nosey suesey handed it to me, with her mouth wide open waiting to hear my answer. Then granny asked another question before I could answer the first one. " How long have you been feeling like this?" I felt like some one had pushed the pause button on me. Then granny said " did you hear what I said?" "yes" but I couldn't remember, so she said we'll talk later!

If I'm pregnant what in the world am I going to do, then I remembered that today was a week day and if I made it to the clinic before 5:00 o'clock I'll find out today if I'm pregnant. So I hurried upstairs pulled out me a sweat suit clean under wear and my white shell tops then headed to the shower to freshen up. After putting on my cloths and jewelry, I looked myself over in the mirror like always but this time I felt ugly. Every thing looks extra big to me, my nose looks like Michelle Jackson, my lips like jay jay , and my eyes chinky like a china doll. I didn't have time to change my cloths so I kept what I had on and told granny that I'll be right back, before I left I asked her did she need me to do any thing before I leave?

I went to the clinic by myself because I don't need no one in my business. I walked straight down 22nd and Diamond to 19th and Diamond made a right walked down to 19th and Burks. When I enter the line was all the way to the door, but it didn't take long before I had reached the window. The reception ask me "do you have a appointment, if not sign the sheet and we'll fit you in as a walk in!" I did just that, as I sat down the different smells of perfume ,cleaning products, and funk had my head spinning. It took about a hour before I was called , Ms Lyons come to team C when I sat down Ms Dawn told me "you just made it ,your my last patient for today." After answering some questions she gave me a cup and told me " take this and fill it with urine then place it on the lab table." Not long after that she came back in the room to tell me that my worst dream came true. " Ms Lyons you are pregnant and your about 3months by going by your last menstrual cycle." "take this paper work over to family planning so they can give you your prenatal pills, good luck and have a good day."

All I could think about was how am I going to tell my grand mother this, better yet how am I going to tell Devin? I know he's going to be mad at me. After getting my pills and follow up apt I left and headed back home to try to tell granny the good or bad news. For some strange reason not one time did I care about how my mom may have felt!

Chapter 8

DHS Is Back!

I've been so busy doing me that I haven't realized that I haven't seen my lil brother Leroy and his twin Rachelle in a couple of days. I needed one of them to go to the store for me, so I went to grand mom room to ask if she saw one of them. She paused for a moment before she gave me the bad news. The whole time she was speaking her voice was shaking. " Some one called D H S and kept reporting your mother continues to come over and still abuse those kids, so they took them and placed them until they get to the bottom of the case .I didn't know how to tell you this with tears running down her face. "Your sister Denay is going to stay with her dad and Sherry I can't do nothing with her any more, plus I think she ran away."

That's when I began to realize that the house has been a bit quiet. I couldn't believe that the rest of my siblings are now separated again. Tee Tee and myself was the only siblings left, instantaneously the tears began to fall.

"Why grand mom, why do we have to live like this? Why can't we be happy like other families?" I asked filled with hurt and anger. " I'm tired of this grandmom , we've been dealing with this since I was lil and now I'm grown and if that lady put her hand on me again I'm going to hit her back. Just thinking about her made me sick, my grand mom notice that I was beginning to stumble and tried to grab me with the lil strength she has left. Grand mom held me as I cried and reashored me how much she loved me and needed me in her life, and that every thing happens for a reason and we must stay strong for the rest of our family. At that moment I felt like this was the best time to let her know that I was expecting a baby. So I said it " How can I be strong when I'm pregnant and don't know if I'm going to keep my baby or not!" Guess what my grand mom said? " I all ready knew it " and whipped my tears from my eyes. "Your going to keep this baby because were going to be fine!" " God makes no mistakes, did you tell Kaseem yet?" " No not yet I figured I'd talk to you first" as I dried my tears for the last time.

One more thing granny said " If you need me to be there with you when you tell him I will?"

Trying to put a smile on my face granny asked me to go get her a glass of ice water and if I did she'll dance at my wedding and started to laugh. I laughed at the thought of her dancing because ,I have never saw that. As I clicked on the lights in the kitchen so I could see clearly, I thank God for giving me the worlds greatest grand mom in the world.

"Trina what's up with you babe your stomach is starting to look kind of round?" Your face is getting fat plus my mom said she been dreaming about fish."Devin said when ever she has that dream some one in her family is pregnant! So he looked me straight in the face and said " babe are you pregnant?" with out a smile on his face. I couldn't lie to him so I said "Yes" and you should have seen the smile on his face, I can truly say I didn't expect that. Your not mad? "No" he said as he pulled me close to him as he sat on the edge of the bed. Then he pulled down the zipper on my pants and placed his lips on my stomach a gave it a

gentle kiss ."Don't put these jeans on any more they are to tight!"
I was as happy as a fag in boys town, now that the only two people
that matters knew I was pregnant, I whore the badge with honor.

After finding out he was now about to become a dad, he
would cut hair all day. He would carry those clippers with him
every where he went, and I mean every where. We could either
be on our way to his house or my house and some one would yell
out clippers stop pass my house to cut me and my boys hair. He
would drop me off and proceed to go make that money.

I never questioned him because his pockets stayed fat, he never came home empty handed. Most of the time he would give me
money to put up because we decided that we needed a place of
our own to raise our new baby, we needed that to happen before
the baby was born.

On this particular day I spent most of my day at Devin house,
his mom decided that it would be ok if I spend a night with them.
The damage was already done, I'm 51/2 months pregnant and
the more time I spend with them the more their beginning to
treat me more like family. Devin had been gone for most of the
day and I guess he forgot that I was there and decided to bring
his friends back to his mom house to chill for a while. The crazy
thing was his boy Tom came over with his girl friend and another
girl was with them. His baby sister and I was sitting on the coach
watching T V when we over heard them talking outside on the
steps. "Is that Devin?" I asked as she leaned over the coach to see
if it was him.

When she turned around she gave me a look that said yes
but you need to see who else he has with him. My heart fell to
the floor when I opened the door and say them coupled up. He
looked like he saw Jesus himself ! Not wanting to be rude I said
" hello" and Tom said " Hi Trina this my girl Shannon" and he
left it like . I look at Devin with a look like I'll kill you. Then he

said " Trina this Shannon girl friend Nicky" I turned my lips up and gave her a look that said what ever followed by another nasty look.

I went back in the house to grab my sweater and sat out side with my man and his so called friends. Now nobody wants to talk. Tom says " we about to leave" and Devin says "he'll walk them to the bus stop, then he had the nerve to tell me he'll be right back!" They all got up and left me standing there by my self, I went in the house sat down and started to cry. I can't believe he thinks I'm that dum, not wanting to say much about her brother Linda just rubbed my back and said "don't worry he'll be back" that wasn't my worry my worry was would I still be here? He didn't come back until 4 hours later and when he did I gave him a peace of my mind, then went upstairs to sleep with his sister Linda.

From that day on things went from bad to worst, if it wasn't some girl it was some women all up n his face. I think he thinks I'm stuck with him now that I'm pregnant. For the most of it he gives me money for the day and I don't see him any more until its time to go to bed. I spend more time with his sisters than him now days and he's the only one happy. Roe is his oldest sister who is now planning my baby shower, she's the big sister I never had. She treats me the same way she treats her younger siblings, if she yells at them she yells at me too.

Everytime I would come to visit Devin he would eventually leave me in the house , this was beginning to annoy me. I decided to stay away for a little while to let him know that I had feelings too, If he didn't want to be with me I'd rather be by my self.

My uncle B cool finally caught me in the house, I haven't seen him in a while even though we live in the same house. His nick name for me is face, why he calls me that I don't know. I tried to walk pass him and wave my hand to say hello, instead he reached out and grab my arm and said "come here face, I don't know if your grand mom told you or not but I'm moving soon" "yes" I said and he said " you don't look excited"

"Since I see your not excited I minds well tell you that my mom is leaving with me." I've made settlement on the house and well be moving in two weeks. My jaw dropped but that wasn't it then he said " I need to know your going with us or if your staying here ok"

I said "yes" and walked away. I can't believe this is happening to me ,I'm trying to gather my thoughts while I make my way to grand moms room. My eyes are already filled with tears so I just came straight out and asked her." So grand mom your leaving me too?" " Why didn't you tell me that I needed to find some where to stay?" Granny said " because you don't! I told your uncle if he didn't allow me to take you with us than I don't want to go!" " Are you going with me or not? You know that I need you." What about Tee Tee is she going with us? "She's older than me and decided that she would stay here with your aunt . Your aunt is moving here when we move, she can use a bigger unit for her family." Granny said " you can always come down to visit, trying to make me feel better.

" How am I going to see Devin, you know uncle B cool not going to let him come over like you do." I think grand mom had enough because she said " listen child we'll cross that bridge when we get to it." Go get you some sleep and tomorrow you can use my credit card to go and get you some bigger cloths to wear, Lord knows you can barley fit those cloths you have on. As I turned to walk away granny noticed my head down and told me to " lift my head before you bump into a wall, acting like you lost your best friend."

I mumbled to myself ,I did and my life if were moving in with the drill Sargent. I didn't really have much of a choice. I couldn't afford to pay my own bills yet and things had changed when it came to me and Devin. The more I thought about it maybe I should leave my past behind so I could see a brighter future. Sitting in the rocking chair in my bed room all I could think about was all the good times I had in this room, the good ones and even the bad.

A strange felling of anticipation came over me, I began to take the bears off my wall and pace them in my laundry bag for safe keeping. That's it for tonight, I'll start packing when I get back from shopping tomorrow. I'll make sure I get some boxes from the corner store. I laid down said my prayers and fell fast asleep.

Everything is packed, Boxes are everywhere. Uncle says" come on face GG brother will be here with the truck in a half hour, make sure you have everything". Mommy all your boxes and your bedroom set is in the living room, Are you sure your not taking your furniture ? All you want is the two chairs from the living room set that you just brought out of everything ?she had she choose the two chairs that looked like old antiques, never mind what I thought they was hers and that's all that matters . Devin didn't even come over to help me pack. I guess he really doesn't care.

The truck is here and this tall dark skinned brother gets out of the

Truck looking like he plays football. And I grabbed one of my the box tears filled my eyes. I didn't want him to see me cry, he grabbed the box saying let me take that from you, your pregnant you get the small things. Aunt Linda was there with her-family waiting for us to move out so that she could move in. Kevin and uncle Tommy were moving so fast. Were done so you and mommy can catch a hack to follow us to the new house I'll show you around the house once we get there,we did as we were told.

GG stayed home setting everything up. I had the middle room next to uncle Tommy room , Grandma had the backroom.

They were unpacking the truck Pretty fast and for some strange reason I kept catching Kevin watching me. If in wasn't already in relationship I would definitely make him mine. I think he has a family, it doesn't matter though because I love Devin.

This is a beautiful home. The living room is long. The dining room is huge it has an opened kitchen and a shed that leads to a great big back yard.

| helped granny unpack her things. I hung her clothes in the closet and placed her under garments in the drawers. I hung her curtains and made her bed. We were all tired so we all got showered and left the rest for the next morning. My bedroom is next to the bathroom, which is good because on the low I'am scared of the dark. I turned on my night light and got in the bed. I had to get used to sleeping in a pitch black house. I already missed the projects. We never had to worry about an electric bill we kept most of the lights on in our house. I. Missed that street light that was outside my old bedroom window. It came on like clock-work every day. It gave me just enough light. No one ever knew I was afraid of the dark and now my secret has come to the surface.

The phone was ringing, I couldn't move as fast as I used to so my aunt ticked up the phone. Yes, she's here. "Trina, Devin wants you on the phone" GG said. Yeah. What's up Trina can you come and spend the weekend with me? I miss you he says. Yes, I responded, the feeling is mutual. " I'll be down at six. I'll meet you at your moms" and then I hung up the phone. I quickly packed my overnight bag. There was no need for pajamas because whenever was with him I slept naked. Easy access I guess and I thought to myself , I'm going to tear that dick up tonight.

I'm finished packing so I go tell granny that I'll see her Sunday night. Its Friday and I washed and ironed her clothes for the next week. Then I filled all of her med slots and separated the morning and night doses for the week. Meals on wheels already delivered the food at twelve this afternoon so she'll be fine. I gave her a kiss and made sure I locked up the house as I was leaving.

The fifteen trolley will take me to 30th and Girard. Then I'll catch the 61 bus it will let me off right on Devin moms block. She lived in the Johnson home projects. As I was turning the corner Devin greeted me with a big hug and a kiss that le me known that he missed me and wanted me bad. He reached down to grab my bag and I could see his manhood growing. That thing right there is so good. I'm long over due and I hope we don't stay too long at his mom house I thought and we didn.t. I said hello to everyone and he gathered our things. We walked through the projects up to strawberry mansion on a small block where his dad lived.

| couldn't believe he was staying in this house. It was not finished. The first floor looked as if they started the work for remodeling and couldn't afford to finish. There were bags of cement lying around. And sheetrock up against the wall. Parts of the floor were weak 'cause it wasn't finished. I must say that the wall where the fire place stood was so nice. It had different types of stones in it. We couldn't stay downstairs so we went up to his bedroom. On our way to his room we passed by his step-dads room, I poked my head in his room and said hello. He waved hello and continued talking on the phone. once I got in Devin room I placed my bags on the floor near the closet and sat down on his full size bed. It wasn't much to his room I guess it's because he just moved in not to long ago. There was no television, but he did have a radio and a small night stand with a little lamp on it with pictures of us. He must have forgotten that he placed our pictures face down. I couldn't understand why, but all I knew was that anger started to build up inside on me. When he realized that I already seen it he tried to play like everything was good. I didn't say anything at first as he dived on top of me trying to fix the pictures at the same time. You know me I cant hold water so I let him have it. I'm

sitting here wishing that I never came here. The thought of him having another girl in his room sitting where I'm

sitting was to much to handle. "How come you keep cheating on me?"" What are you talking about Trina?" He had some nerve as if' Iam stupid. I saw you fix the pictures. "I was cleaning my room and forgot to it" he said. Yeah ok I said. We argued all night. I never got a chance to show him, how much I missed and wanted him. Instead we slept with a line through the middle of us. I dared him to cross that line. I hate this nigga…. I'm going to show him better than I can tell him ,right after I have his baby.

Chapter 9

SPENDING TIME WITH MY HOMEGIRLS

*I*t's like there is a bug in the air, every one of my home girls and I are pregnant the same time, but we all due in different months. It's kind of strange all of a sudden Kia and I are getting very close. Devin and I decided to ask kia to be our son Godmom. This decision was based on how sweet she has been to me. Being the perfect friend in my time of trouble. When I think about it I can't believe this is the same girl that I use to argue with all the time in school. I love this girl because she keeps it real with me, no matter how mad I get with her even if we stop speaking. I don't worry about it because will be speaking again in a few days like nothing has ever happen. She's big and pregnant just like me, and we both had the craving for some crabs . We went to get some from the crab shack on the corner of 26th Glenwood, and went back to her boy friend house to eat them where she lives at. Her baby father is a DJ so she played some of his records as we sat out side on the front steps eating and talking about how we planed on repaying them back for how them niggas treated us while we where pregnant. We laugh so hard and gave each other a high five, because deep down inside we both knew we was telling the truth. Kia was so bored that she asked me if she could do my hair? Of course I said " yes" She did my hair in a sculptor ponytail, handed me the mirror to see if I like it. I checked it very carefully and to my surprise I love it! I gave her a couple of dollars and reminded her that for now on she was my new hair dresser. Then I told her how much I appreciated her, from that day on we promised each other that if we ever ran into some money we would open up a hair salon together one day. Believe it or not she had the nerve to write it on a peace of paper, and we both signed it with our crazy selves. As soon as her boyfriend came home ,the whole atmosphere changed. It seems like he erks her soul, but never the less minds does the same thing to me. To take her mind off her problems we started dancing off some of the music that she played. We reminisced about the shows we used to do at the Recreation Center, before you knew it time stared flying. Kia talked her boy friend into walking us to William Dick school yard so that I could go over Devin house. That was half way to his house, I gave them both a hug and thanked them for walking me and also for the good time I had with them.Kia said she would call me during the week. At this point in my pregnancy you minds well say I now live with his mom .I'm there every weekend and they love it, no matter what time I showed up to their was always so type of excitement going on. His big sister Roz was the best she couldn't wait for her niece or nephew to come. I could tell because she had already brought cloths, a crib and a stroller, if I didn't know better I think this was her baby. Devin came in at 12:00 brought me my usual a cheese steak a bag of plain chips and a pepsi soda, right after we ate we went straight to bed.

Mr. Aaron came over Devin mom house today. I didn't expect to see him out of all people in the world he came pass to see me. " Hi Trina I came over to let you know that section 8 is excepting applications, if you want to go with me I'll take you with me". I forgot to tell you that when your done Ms. Clair going to have your application pulled. I didn't believe him but I went alone and said "yes" He said " make sure you bring your proof of Ide and your proof of income alone with your social security card with you." I quickly graded my things and we left. I never knew that this man talked so much, he wrapped my head off. I looked out the window trying block him out by the sounds of the cars that passed by, even that didn't work so I pretended like I was listening by saying umm hum or yes. What I did hear was we're here as he stop the car, we both stepped out of the station wagon. The office was very small located on the lower level of a duplex building located of 53rd and Market. " Hi my name is Trina and I'm here to fill out a application, the lady shocked my hand and gave me a application to fill out. It took me about 20 minutes to finish the application and I was done. She quickly went over my paper work then she said " You didn't put down your source of income!" I said that I was on public assistance and I received $158.00 every two weeks plus $265.00 in food stamps" Then she told me that I need two months rent and one month security. Are you ready for this ? my rent will be $41.oo dollars a month so all together you'll need $123.00 at the end of the month There will be a $25.00 dollar deposit to get the keys to look at the apartment, if you have it now you can go and look at it ,if you like it we can get started today? Before I could answer Mr. Aaron said " yes she does " and reached over to hand her the money. Oh one more thing "I need your drivers license to make a copy of it ?" The address is 3416 Haverford Ave apt 403 its and efficiency, you can stay their until your baby come and then we'll move you into a 1 bedroom apt. I can't believe that my dreams was coming true, Mr.Jennifer said it shouldn't take you guys no more than 2hours to take a look at it and hand me the keys.

She was right we made it there in no time ,it was right next door to the fire station, I felt good about that. The first thing I noticed was the beautiful landscaping as I turned the key to the front door the mail boxes was located to the right side of the apt for all of the residents in the complex . We finally made it to the apt 403, I took a deep breath and turn the door knob. It was wall to wall brand new carpet on the floor, a large window in the middle of the living room next to the small kitchen. On the right side of the front door is the hallway that had a walk in closet directly across from the door. Down the hall to the left is a full size bathroom, just the right size for me not to big or to small. The kitchen had brand new cabinets and new appliance ,I opened every cabinet to make sure they worked properly. I turned to look at Mr. Aaron and said I love it, "Alright lets go back to the office to let them know you want it." Before leaving I turned around and gave him a big hug to let him know how much I appreciate him.

When we got back to the office she had already checked my references." Do you like it "

Mrs. Clair asked "Yes mam " I replied. " Well I guess it's yours , when can you bring in your down payment?" Mr. Aaron reached in his pocket and pulled out a knot of money and paid for it. I couldn't believe it , I was smiling from ear to ear. Mrs. Clair gave me a receipt and placed the keys in my hands. I had to sign a couple more papers and signed my lease, we was out. This time on the whole ride back I rapped his head off, I guess pa back is a mother. I love this man right now more than ever before, I had to calm myself down before I have a heart attack. Just think about it, this morning I woke up barely homeless, and know at the age of 19 teen years old with my own apartment. A smirk came across my lips and I closed my eyes and gave my Lord and savior thanks for the door he has opened for me and my child. Oh and for the people he has placed in my life.

Devin and I are so excited about our new apartment, the only thing that I haven't had the heart to do yet was tell my

grandmother and my uncle B cool. We've been paying on our living room set, and going back and forth to our apartment hanging up pictures, hanging our curtains in the bathroom trying to have every thing done before our baby come. Our colors for décor is cream, pink and black, most of the time Devin goes up there by himself because the baby will be here any day now.

Their was so many times I thought about just calling my grand mom to give her the bad news. Then I realize that that would make me a coward, my grandmother always told me if you have something to say to some one, say it to their face and stare them in the eye to let them know that you mean every word you say, there for their will be no miss understanding. My heart ache at the thought of telling her but I have to do it, I'll let her know tonight to pick up a few of my things. I called my homie Derick to ask him to take me home latter, I don't care what time I call him he never says No. Derick used to live three doors down from me on 22nd Diamond. I don't think Devin feels threaten by him because of his weight, but only if he knew like I knew he would be, because he can have any girl he wants and I really mean it. He has money for days and cars to drive for any occasion, he's like heavy Dee of the projects. All the girls around the way want him even though they know he has a main girl friend. When I think about it I'm kind of ignorant my self for calling him all times of the night and no matter what he still comes, that's why he'll always have a special place in my heart.

I've been waiting on this phone so long that , I forgot the phone was in my hand. Just when I was about to give up he picks up. " yo what up" he said trying to be smart " now what you want me to do" Derick said with out me even saying who I was. Tring to be sexy using my sexy voice, I said I hate those

Dam caller ID. "What man, do you want and can you just get to the point?" " Can you please come get me and take me to uncle B cool house to get my cloths?" Give me a half and hour and I'll be there" he said. Thanks big daddy I said and we hung up. Just like clock work he came right on time just as he said, then I heard the horn beep I quickly grabbed my coat and we was out. He drives like a bat out of Hell and before you could even blink your eyes good, we was there. " Give me my money!" with his hand held out.

I leaned over and gave it a slap and said don't leave me I be right back. " Girl you play to much, hurry up because I got to make!" He said. " Ok" I said and gave him the puppy dog look before leaving, he couldn't resist that look.

My aunt and uncle was already upstairs in their bedroom like I thought they would be, good I said to myself and head-ed straight to my grand moms room. She's still sitting up on the side of her bed, so greeted her with a kiss on her cheek. " Mommy do you need your cloths wash and iron?" " Yes and I need my credit cards and life insurance bill paid, if you have time?" Then she said it," Where have you been, I haven't seen you in a while?" Well mommy " I just got my own apartment, its here in West Philly real close to you and all I have to catch is one bus. The 31 bus lets me off at the end of your block on 63rd and Haverford. I moved to 34th and Haverford, so it'll be easy for me to still have time to come over to pay your bills and wash and iron your cloths for the week and also set your meds up for the week." Never stopping to take a breath I kept on talking. " Mommy I don't want to raise my baby up in uncle B cool house, I'm about to become 20 years old and I need my own space!" I said and the tears began to roll down her face. " What am I going to do with out you?" " I can't live with out you, I had hoped that I would be dead before you left me!" she said with tears still coming, I couldn't believe my ear. " Don't say that mommy, I love you and can't live with out you neither and I wont. I'll be here every week to help you ,I promise you and wiped her face." " Mommy your in good hands now you live in a safer neighbor hood and plus God has blessed you with a wonderful daughter in law who loves you just as much as I do." I begged her to give me a smile before I grabbed my cloths to leave. " I kissed her one more time and reashored her that I would return on Friday to help her take care of her bills. As I made my way down the steps I prayed that Derrick haven't left me.

This pain is coming faster than a local motor train. On this particular day I couldn't seem to stop running back and forth to the bathroom. as unusual Devin is out cutting hair or hanging out with the boys. His big sister Reesie keeps me moving, walking to the market or shopping for cloths for the baby. I have never been in the thrift store before, but the more I go out with Reesie the familiar I'm becoming with shop-ping for less. While I shuffle through the cloths I realize that theirs some very nice things these white folks donate to the thrift store. We as black folks are to ignorant to go inside to purchase, or just fearful of someone seeing us come out of the store. The more I walked the stronger the pain , I reached out to Roz and said " wait my back is hurting and I feel pain in my lower part of my stomach!" "Ok" Reesie said "let me get these sheets for the baby crib and we can leave!" After leaving the store we caught the 61 bus to head back home

" Why do it feel like my vagina is dropping?" In a very calm tone , Roz said "you might be going in labor." If this is what labor pains feels like, it hurts like hell. Soon as we got in the house I was told to relax, and I tried to do just that because that was a order from Mrs Renay. Time was moving rapidly after dinner I called myself lying down to try to ease the pain but I kept running back and forth to the bathroom feeling as if I have to take a dump. At this point Reesie can't take it any more and tells me to get my bag so we can go to the hospital. " no I can't...I have to wait for Devin,, so he can be their when the baby come!"

It's about 10:30 at night and he's still not here yet , when all of the sudden I fell to my knees and my water broke. I screamed at the top of my lungs . I can't take it no more Roz! Just as we was on our way out the door guess who walks in? My Baby Devin, filled with excitement he grabbed my bag as we waited for the ambulance to come." Roz the ambulance is here" Mrs Renay said " Reesie you and I are going to meet yall at the hospital."

I don't know why but at this moment just looking at Devin is making me sick. I calling him every thing but a child of God. Soon as we enter into Temple Hospital the doctors took me straight to the back to Labor ward. They placed a I ve in my arm, to start the procedure ,doctors are coming from every where even my mid wife is here. I don't even remember how to breath correctly, because the pain is coming so fast. Things are happening so fast I don't remember me taking off of my cloths, but what I do know is that my legs are cocked open with all of my goodies showing. I don't care at the moment. My mouth is dry and my lips are cracked from breathing so hard, Devin try's. I frustrated yelling "this mother F in baby is killing me and I want it out!" Now I'm screaming " get the doctor its coming" and I start pushing. When the nurse came she said " Mrs Lyons wait, stop pushing." " I can't and kept pushing and I dam near passed out as I gave it all I had. I almost flipped off the back of the bed. Then I heard it plop and the baby was out, the baby was out. The doctors rushed to clean the baby mouth and nose so the baby can breath clearly, as I took a glance at the baby tears began to roll down my face. Devin leaned in and gave me a kiss on my dry lips and said we done it Babe's ,it's a beautiful baby Boy.

Theirs no grater feeling than to hold the child that you felt growing on the inside of you finally looking at you face to face, was mind blowing to me. After all of the excitement was over his aunty and grandmother got a chance to hold the baby. We all stared at the new addition to the family, I thank God for a healthy baby with all of his digits and body parts in its proper place. The baby was born at 5:30 am weighing 5 pounds 6 oz. everyone left except Devin, then he promised me from this point on we would be a family forever. Devin laid down beside me in the hospital bed and held me as we both fell asleep.

There is nothing like the fresh smell of a new place and new furniture. I'm starting to think that may be Devin has been over here setting things up for us because the apartment looks so nice. Our baby is now 1 month, we couldn't leave his moms house until our son had his first check up, you know how the older folks act."lol" My body doesn't hurt as much as it used to, Devin wasn't taking any chance of me having a set back. "Babe's I'll set the cloths up in the dresser and hang the cloths up in the closet while you sit down and get some rest!" I did just that , he even cooked diner for us. When diner was done we ate and watched a movie underneath the dimed light n hopes that the baby would sleep for more that a ten minute nap.

The baby slept all day and night long , because he had a bottle before I put him down after his bath. That gave Devin and I a chance to reconnect with each other. that Devin is working out more as I rubbed my hands across his now rock hard chest. When he begin to run his hands across my use to be flat stomach, he whisper in my ear that " you need to work out with me to get rid of this stomach. . It's starting to get on my nerves, but I pretend not to hear him just to keep the arguments down.

I try not to complaint any more because he has changed the way he acts since the baby has been home, he's home every night and I love it.I feel like we are a happy family most of the time, at least I know he truly loves his son with all his heart. My mom doesn't care to much for him she says " Devin is so sneaky! and is not good enough for me. I don't care what she or anyone else says about him. I love him and my son ,this is my family now and I'm going to do whatever I have to do to keep it!

The next morning I decided to get up to make breakfast and realized that we was out of eggs, so I slipped on something to run across the street to the store. As I went to walk through the front doors to the apartment building, I noticed a couple of young ladies sitting outside on the steps. As I grew closer to them I waved my hand and said hello to them as I excused myself so that I could walk pass with out a problem.

They didn't think that I heard them as they whispered who is she to each other? One of them said " I think she's the girl who moved in with that guy on the 3rd floor." Now I'm on my way back from the store and their still talking, "she don't look like the same girl that I see with him." I pretended not to hear her, now I'm thinking to myself that I should curse his black ass out; but things are going to good for me to say something right now.

I never even looked back at them as I shut the door to the apartment building.

I know this is weird but I counted each step as I made my way to the apartment, just as I went to open the door. Devin was standing there bag in his hands ready to leave, he leaned in and gave me a kiss and said "I have heads to cut down North Philly" He kissed his son and said "my ride is out side waiting for me."

As I stood there stuck for a minute I thought to myself I didn't see nobody in a car outside. I sure didn't see any of his friends, I tried to stop thinking so hard because now I'm thinking about what I just heard and I'm getting angry. Their goes the plan I had for breakfast and by now I've lost my appetite. So I option out for a chance to eat for a couple of minutes to sit down to watch television. The baby had already went to sleep in his play pin, and before I knew it I had falling back to sleep. When I woke up it was 2:00 clock pm. I couldn't believe he wasn't back yet so I decided to call his moms house to see if he had stopped over their for a minute. No one answered the phone so I hug up and decided I'll just wait until he comes home. I reached in the play pin to wake up Booboo so I could get him dressed and spend so time with him. I didn't go outside because I didn't know anyone from the building yet. We played with his lil toys and watched baby shows like Barny until I couldn't take it anymore. Time flew by so fast that I had cooked dinner, washed the baby up and fed him his bottle before he was laid down for bed.

Still no phone call from Devin, not wanting to , I reached over to grab the phone of the coffee table to call his moms house one more time. This time it was now almost 2:oo am, I felt so bad for calling his mom house this late but I had to make sure he was alright. Ms Rose picked up "Hello who is this " with sternness in her voice. ," Ms Rose its Trina sorry for calling so late but is Devin there?" " No Baby I haven't seen Devin all day but if he comes in I'll have him call you!" I said "ok thanks" I'm thinking see this is the stuff that I be talking about with him. I'm going to sit up and wait right here so that I can see what time he comes in this apartment, I grabbed my pillow and blanket and laid right on the coach. I'm wondering what fantastic lie is he going to come up with. What ever it is it better be a good one. I need to talk to my best friend but its to late, I'll call her in the morning ,and I laid there until I finally went to sleep

Time waits for no one, so I decided to keep things movin

oving plus I haven't heard from that jack ass since yesturday. I'll handle him when ever I see him, and I'm not callng around looking for him anymore! I have a child to think about right now who needs me , so I grabed the baby and begand to feed him and dressed him after wards. When I was done I placed him in thre swing so I could clean the apartment. When ever I get in the mood to clean I listen to the radio, my favorite station is Power 99 fm. You would have thought that the sound of music would have helped but it didn't.

I'm thinking to myself but speaking out loud, my life is filled with so many ups and downs, just as it seems as if things are getting better Devin always finds a way to " F" things up again. I know he's cheating on me but I don't have the proof to prove it ! What's in the dark will come to the light. The music is thumping and for a moment I began to allow myself to forget about my problems, the next thing I before I knew it I was performing for my baby. The smile that showed up on his lil face was priceless. At that moment I decided that living for this precious gift from God was more important to me than anything else in this world. Than all of a sudden I hear the phone ring, I tried to take my time to answer the phone just in case it may have been Devin. I didn't want to seem desperate . " Hello" I said " Dag girl why you answer the phone like that?"

Kia said, In return I answered " I thought you was Devin., He stayed out last night and I haven't heard from him yet but it cool because I'm telling him that he has to leave!" " Girl if you don't calm down and think about what you do before you say something your going to regret, talking out of the side of your mouth!"

Kia said and when I turned to look at lil Dee, he was fast asleep looking just like his father. I thought about what she had just said and said " girl your right but I'm so tired of this Kia" and the tears began to roll. " Well girl I called to tell you my problems but after hearing yours, I see that we're in the same boat!" Kia said and we both began to laugh.

"Wait girl I hear him turning his key now, I'm not going to say nothing to him" is what I managed to get out of my mouth before he interrupted me with that lame ass hello Babes. I pretended not to hear him and rolled my eyes at him and continued to talk in a low and sexy voice; trying to pretend that I'm talking to some dude.

" I'll talk to you later " is what I told Kia" "ok" is what she said followed by " don't get yourself beat up !" and we both laugh before hanging up the phone.

Maybe he needs to think that I'm talking to some one else since he's not thinking at all. He went straight to the bathroom to take a shower but before he did so he placed his money on the entertainment center. I guess he want me to think that he was doing hair all this time. I went over and broke myself off a lil something , I figured if he stayed out all night I minds well get paid too. When he got out of the shower and changed into some sweatpants and a T shirt he sat down beside me and never said a word about where he been, and neither did I ask him. He got up to grab his money and had this puzzle look on his face but he knew not to ask me about it for fear of me tearing into his ass, so he placed what was left in his pocket and sat his ass back down.

On this particular day I'm home alone as usual, on this day I decided to open my apartment door as I clean and listen to my music. I guess my neighbor had the same idea as I did because I could clearly hear her music over mine. I turned my music off and decided to listen to hers instead, plus she was listening to my favorite singing group S W V. It sounded so good that I went to the door to hear a lil better, that's when I noticed that their was no instruments being played in the back round. Then out of no where one off the girls walked to the front door chasing this beautiful lil baby who was crawling out the door, just before she grabbed her .she caught me listening . I tried to play it all and said Hello, she came over to me and introduced herself. "My name is Nell and yours" "My name is Trina, is that you in their singing?" she said " Yes it's me and my sisters" I told her that they sounds good and ended the conversation but before her sisters left she stop by my house and introduced her sisters to me.

Later on that night we all went outside and sat in the front of the apartment building. That's when I met the rest of the young ladies that I saw a couple of months ago.

Their name was Joanna, Tammie, Renay,Robin and you already me Nelly. I smiled at her because she sounds kind of silly, but we had so much fun it felt like I knew them for ever. When Devin came home I just grabbed my son and wave good bye. I had all ready knew what to do from previous experience, he felt like he shouldn't have to tell me to leave my , I should already now to do so. I hated that about him. He didn't say to much to them I guess it was in fear that some one would slip up and say something about his lil secret he was keeping. I could tell they had something on him by the way they looked at him , like I can't stand you lil dirty dog look!

He let me know that he don't like me hanging out with them girls, when I asked why we began to argue and the next thing I knew we was fighting rite in front of my son. I guess it was the sound of the baby crying that caused us to stop. I reached out to grab my baby with tears n my eyes and hugged him tightly to try to ease his pain. I can't be going through this in front of my son all the time and plus he keep telling me he's gong to stop fighting on me and he still haven't changed. These are the thoughts that's running through my mind as I try to get myself together. I telling myself he'll try to give me money or buy flowers or jewelry the next day to make up but its not working any more.

Later on that night after I put the baby down to sleep, like clock work he try's to have sex with me and like a foul I let him.

I notice that he's even making love to me different, he dragging and flipping me around like a rag doll. He's trying to pick me up and walk with me while having sex, he's acting like I'm a skinny girl and dam near killed the both of us. He's out of breath and I'm out of breath this is to much dam work , we both lay their dripping in sweat as I gazed in his eyes wondering what ever happen to my best friend.

Chapter 10

DEVIN LEAVES!

I'm two years deep in this shit, my son in now 2years old and thing still haven't changed. My cousin and I are on our way to my grand moms house so I can do her bills and wash her cloths for her. Nia spent the night with me so she could keep me company at grand mom house. Just as we where on our way out the door Nelly knocks on the door. I opens the door and the first thing she says is " Trina why I see your car on 54th Haverford?" " do you know somebody down that way?" I said "are you sure?" "girl I know your car it's always parked out front." She said and guess what she was right. I asked her if she felt like taken me back up their so I could retrieve my car? She said " give me a minute, meet me down stairs I need to get something." Now my stomach is hurting and my heart starts to racing. I didn't know what to expect when I got their neither did I know how I would react if I saw something I didn't want to see. What I did know was that I was taking my car with my extra set of keys.

Nelly is back so I jumped in the front seat and Nia took the back seat. We talking shit to each other and then Nelly informs me that he was their all night because she seen the car their last night and in the morning while she was leaving. Then she stops and say " there it is on the right hand side of the street." I thanked her and told her I'll give her something later, then I motioned Nia to grab my bag and we quietly opened the car door, started the car and we was out. I cant believe this dude ill see how he going to react when he has to walk all the way home.

I was so mad that I cursed all the way back to the apartment, I was even madder because I had to break a promise that I made to with my grand mom but I had to handle my business first. I want out of this relationship and soon as I walked in the apartment door , I reached for the trash bags and started grabbing and bagging his cloths. The strange thing is this time I didn't cry, we had already started loading his bags in the car. My plans was to take his cloths to his mother house and leave them their. Here I go talking shit to my cousin saying "this no good nigger got the nerve to take our car to his new chick house and chill with her!" This time their was no responds back, I noticed that my cousin came back in the door with the very same bag she left out with, and dropped it right on the floor with out saying a word. Her lips was moving but I couldn't' hear a word, I guess she was saying here comes Devin.

Devin didn't even care that my cousin was sitting on the couch. When I turned around his face was filled with anger and sweat. I never saw her so scared, she hurried and sat down like she had no part in it, with her punk ass. Believe it or not I was scared to but I had to keep my anger face on, he had sweet dripping down his face and his lips was white, I think that came from him licking his lips while his thirsty ass walked all the way home. When he finally walked through the door he stood their staring at me looking like the incredible Hulk. lol

"Trina what the fuck is your problem?" "Why the fuck you take the car?" he didn't give me a chance to answer." I should knock your fucking head off." He said all of this in just one breath. Devin didn't even care that my cousin was sitting on the coach and neither did I. When I say he cursed me out and called me every thing you could think about saying ,he said it. So I said it " You didn't think about me when you was over your B house last night , and driving her around in our car did you?" " I'm so tired of argueing with you, if you don't want to be here any more than won't you just Leave!" I couldn't' believe that I just said it. His responds to that blew my mind, he said " your right I tired of this bull shit and I don't want to be here any more." He looked me straight in my face when he said it, and at that moment I knew that it was over. This new chick had stolen his heart and the tears rolled down my face non stop. Every thing in me wanted to grab him and beg him to stay but deep down I knew it was for the best.

He looked around and noticed that his things was already packed, that when he asked me if I was going to take him down his moms house? In the process of us calming down ,we both realized that we had a lot to loose because we both paid for every thing together. I know that this will take yall by surprise but I decided to let him take the car and I would keep every thing in the apartment. I gave him the keys to the car and sat down beside Nia and watched him pack the rest of his things to load up in the car. I almost forgot to get my keys to the apartment before he left. He place them in my hand and we said good bye.

Before he left he turned around and said " I wasn't at my girl-friend house I was at my cousin Bee Bee house." I sat their with the what if look on my face.

I can't help but wonder at times if I did the right thing. I miss him like crazy, I'm starting to think that if I cold have just a lil piece of him is better than not having no part of him at all. My son keeps waiting up for his daddy to show up at night, and he never comes. Now that he's gone all I seem to remember is the good times we used to share. It's as simple as just waiting for Devin Finish working out so I can lay my head down working out so I could lay my head down on his chest to listen to his heart beat. While at the same time admiring the way his deodorant smelled as it blended in with his natural body sent, it might sound strange but that turned me on. Then he would flex his muscles and say Trina look at these guns, and we both would bust out in laughter. God help me ,how am I going to make it with out him I thought to myself.

My son needs his father and I want my man back! I decided that I would get dressed and go to his Mom's house to get him. First I had to call my brother over to watch his nephew. I promised that if he would watch him tonight that he could bring his girl friend too. He said " Yes" It's a Friday night and I hope I can catch him. My brother showed up at about 8:00 pm. I'm already dressed looking good and smelling good, and I forgot to mention that I already have a new car, so I grab my keys and kiss my son good night before leaving.

I'm driving practicing the things that I'm going to say to him when I see his face. When I get to his moms house he was listening to music while he was getting dress. "Hi Ms Rose is Devin here?" I asked " yes baby he's upstairs getting dress" she said. I excused myself and went upstairs and from the site of things he looks very happy, he's singing while he's cutting his own hair. I stood their for a while just watching him before I had enough and decided to touch him on the shoulder to let him know that I was their. To my surprise he gave me the biggest hug and kiss, than he asked me how was I doing? I thought this was the perfect opportunity to tell him how much I miss him and wanted him back in my life, also how much I wanted him to please come back home.

His responds was " Trina I like it better the way that things are, I'm happy plus we get alone better now." I didn't even realize that I was now on my knees crying and begging him to give his family another chance. He grabbed me to lift me off the floor. Then he wiped the tears from my eyes and told me for the last time that it was over. I had no choice but to get myself together and grab my things and go. As I went to say goodnight to Ms Rose she called me into the kitchen and said " Listen baby don't you ever let a man tear you down ,you put all your time and energy into you and your baby. I want you to go back to school to further your education. When you find out exactly what you want to do let me know and I'll help you with lil Devin ok!" She gave me a motherly hug and a kiss on the cheek and reminded me how much she loved me. " You're a good woman and you deserve better, Devin still wants to play. He's my son but I'm still a women."

When I left her house I was in no mood to be alone so I went to my girlfriend house Asha Tay. From the looks of things nothing has changed, not even the company she keeps. My heart was truly broken but I didn't trust her enough to share my feelings so I kept them to myself. I waited for her to finish getting dress so we could walk down the street to the bar. Just like old times we rolled up a dutch and smoked it before going to the bar. Asha gave me the 411 on every thing I had miss since I haven't been around as much. WE was feeling nice right about now, so when we got in the bar I order me a Long island Ice tee. When I scoped the room I saw the same faces that I use to see at the dollar party. I had no problem with finding a dance partner, we danced so much and had such a good time ,before I knew it ,it was time for the bar to close.

Even though I had a good time my heart was still hurting from rejection. I vowed from that night on to never fall for these niggas again. I would just freak them and move on treat them like they treat us. When I do settle down the man would have to be about 5 years older than me and can't have any children. One more thing I don't want no more around the way dudes.

I never made it back home that night because I was to high to drive, so I stayed at my aunt house instead, wrapping my cousin head off about what happened until we both fell asleep.

After having my heart broken to pieces on the night before. I hurried home to releave my brother from babysitting duty, before I left I washed my face and brushed my teeth and thanked my aunt for letting me stay the night before I left. I almost couldn't remember where I left my car at, Then I remembered that I had to walk down to Asha Tay house to retrieve it. I just wanted to go lay down and cuddle up with the one and only true man of my life, my baby boy. I turned the key to open the door. My son was dressed in his pj's playing on the floor with his cars. As soon as he saw me he jumped up in my arms as if he hadn't seen me in months. It's just what I needed. My brother was ready to go so I gave him a little extra cash, 'cause staying overnight was not part of the plan. He smiled, gave me a hug, high fived his nephew, and said call me again when you need me.

If I didn't know better I would've thought that I was being set up. No more than a half hour had passed when the phone started ringing. The first time I answered someone hung upon me. I decided to keep the phone near me so that could answer on the first time. The phone rings again, I answered it and a woman says, "can I please speak to Katrina"? This is she, I say. I knew that it couldn't be someone from my family or a friend 'cause they all call me Trina or Suggie "I don't know if you can hear me or not, but my name is Nicky. No bells went off in my head and I had a feeling that I wasn't going to like where this was headed. No I don't, I say. I met you one night in front of Devin mom's house. I was with Don and his girlfriend. I remember you were pregnant I'm starting to remember now and in pissed. With a stern voice I say, yeah and that's when she says, "well Devin and I have been dating ever since. I've been going to y'all apartment to spend some nights with him. I can tell you how your apartment looks from the moment you enter the front door to the finishes you have on the bathroom wall. I. Couldn't believe it. So I said if this is true then tell me. She says, well apparently you love your family because the wall that faces your front door is full of family pictures. Your living room set is rose pink. Your color theme is cream, black and pink. I stopped her in her tracks and asked, what the hell are you calling mer. I wanted to tell you this for a while but Devin kept stopping me. He hasn't been with me for a couple days so I decided to call you Trina.

" Well fuck you, you no good bastard, don't call me anymore or I'll break your face whenever I see you, I yelled. You wanted him now you got him. No, you dont understand Devin said ya'll wasn't together, he just helped you out while you were pregnant, but I kept catching him in a lie.

Well that's your problem 'cause I don't care, I said as I hung up the phone.

Now I'm crying in front of my 'lil man. He's sitting on my lap and wipes my tears with his little hand. I guess it was a sign from God to let me know that everything would be all tight. I gave him a hug and told him how much I loved him. I told him to continue to play with his toys while I made him some lunch. After he ate his lunch he took a nap, then I remembered that I hadn't taken a shower yet with everything that was going on. I grabbed my towel and shower cap and slid it on my head. Before I jumped in the shower I looked at myself in the mirror and promised that from this point on I would eat right and take care of my body. I jumped in the shower and let the water run down my face as I cried for the last time.

As I sit on the couch watching television a commercial catches my attention. It felt like they were talking directly to me. It's a hair school, Gordon Phillips. I quickly wrote down the phone number and gave them a call. My appointment was made for the following week. I called Ms. Rose to let her know if that offer was still good. Filled with excitement she couldn't stop telling me how proud of me she was. She asked me when is my appointment? I told her it was October 12, at 10 a.m. The year was 1992. Bring him over the night before so you won't be late, she said. Yes ma'am, thank you, I said. I haven't been this excited in a couple of months now. Because of the good news I decided that my son and I would have pizza tonight since it was his favorite. When I told him about the pizza he got so happy." Mommy can we watch a movie too?" "ok" I said. He grabbed the lion king. He would watch that movie so much I knew every line by heart. Then he would get jealous and say "mommy it's not for you, "and I would laugh so hard, when ever he would say that I would get up to leave him to his own party.

I started working out more and cutting back on my food intake, so I just ordered a small pizza. Instead of eating my regular two slices, I decided to only have one slice. I would order juice instead of soda, trying to cut back on the caffeine. If I would have known that Devin wanted a skinny girl, he could have just told me. I don't want to see him amy more until I get my body in shape to where I'm happy hell see me and regret the day that he cheated on me and left his family. I said to myself as I managed to pull myself up for the last sit up.

The pizza man is her ,Lil Devin yield out to me to let me know the bell was ringing. I went to the bell to buzz him in.I could see that he was out of breath from walking up all of those stairs. I asked him for the amount of my food bill again since I couldn't remember the exact amount.

$10.25 he said. I gave him $ 15.25 cents and waved for him to keep the change. My little man grabbed the bottle of juice and shut the door, he already knew where to sit and that was at his little table that sat infront of the window. "Mommy is my daddy coming over tonight?" " No", I said but you can see him at grand moms house when ever you want to. After dinner we both sat down on the couch to continue watching the trest of the movie. Before I knew it he was fast asleep with drawl dripping down the side of his face. I grabbed one of his wipes out of the container to wipe his face off. I didn't want to wake him up so I decided to place a blanket over him and let him sleep right where he was. I felt kind of lonely so I called my bestfriend to talk to her for a while. I slid under the covers at the other end of the couch. The phone rang so long I forgot that I was waiting and I started singing Mary J B song while waiting for her to answer, You abandoned me ...love don't live here amy more". Hello, girl stop making all that noise in my ear" Kia yelled

"What's stunting your bloomers, I asked? " "Girl nobody feels like playing with you, what do you want ?"me knowing my friend I knew that something waswrong. I stopped playing and asked, "what's wrong with you?" " just called me at the wrong time, bill and me just got finish fighting and we broke up. I'm leaving and I'll call you when I Get settled!" I felt so bad all I could say was sorry, I'll wait for your call". When I hung up I sat there and cried thinking what's going on with these men just giving up on their family. I had nothing else to do so, I start praying for her family and mine. I prayed that god would give us the strength to be good single parents. My heart is so heavy now, I went down to the other end of the couch and layed with my son, kissed his forehead and whispered in his ear "I love you son"." I love you too mommy", he said. That's when I realized that what my grand mom said was true. "That all shut eyes are not sleeping". I smiled because it made me feel good

To know that he even loves me in his sleep.

What's going on in the world? It's like their' s a spirit hovering over Philadelphia. The spirit of dump your baby mother. I couldn't even finish washing my son up good with out the phone ringing off the hook. I tried to hurry and wrap my son up in his bath towel and run to answer the phone at the very same time,

when I noticed what I was doing, the poor. Child was being dragged through the hall. He held on to one end and I had the other, " hello" I said. Trina this kitta, she said." What's up girl you not going to believe this, bub and me broke up last night." I couldn't believe it, so I told her about Kia and Bill. She was so upset and kept crying so hard , I don't think she even heard me.

As we continued talking on the phone I finished getting boo boo dressed so I could make him breakfast. I'm so upset over all this nonsense now; I'm *Cursing and shit I completely forgotten that my son was in the room, until he said "Eww mommy you said a bad word!" I said" sorry" and walked into the hall way to finish our conversation. Tiny asked me if she could stay over to my place for the weekend? I told her that it was ok and also asked if her son was coming with her? Her answer was "No" I tried to make her laugh by saying " If I didn't know any better, I would have thought that our baby daddy's planed to dump us all at the same time." She found no hummer in that at all ! We said our goodbyes to one another, my son wanted to go out side to ride his motor cycle and plus I needed some fresh air.* When ever he would ride his bike it would tire this lil boy out. While I was locking the front door to my apartment, I could hear my new girl friend Nelly yelling at her baby father she said " Bi**h you can leave because I don't care anymore"! Then he yield in her face " move so I can leave" . I didn't want to appear to be nosy so I continued what I was doing never looking back at them and proceeded down the steps. You could still hear them yelling Nelly scream " give me my keys!" He threw them and I guess when she tried to get them he ran out the door and right pass me laughing like it was funny.

My bad Trina he yelled as he kept running almost knocking me down trying to get away from her. All I could think about was Dam another relationship that bites the dust. It's a shame that our children are now going to suffer from a broken family home. I sat down on the steps and watch my son ride up and down the street on his bike without a care in the world, I pray that my son will grow up to be a strong man who will always respect his family enough to never leave them. I also asked God to give me the strength to continue to make the best out off the situation that I was now in.

While I was doing all of this praying , I never noticed that my son was now off his bike sitting on the bench talking to the fire man. From the looks of thing he was very comfortable with the man, like he talked to him once before. I didn't want him to be a bother to the man so I went to get him. I reached my hand out to shake the man hand and introduced myself to him. Lil devin said that's my mommy so fast before I could get a word out. I did hear him say " my name is James" and shook my hand.

He informed me that I had a very bright young man, an said " he talks to me all the time, he had a better conversation with him more than he did with some adults". Than he let me know that what ever I was doing with him to keep up the good work because it shows. I thanked him and we both went back up the street. Even though I was impressed with the good news that I just heard, I scold him about sitting down and talking to strangers. Then he reminded me that Mr James wasn't a stranger, mommy he's the fire man who help save people from a fire. I couldn't be mad a him , I just warned him that every body are not nice people, some times fox comes in sheep clothing. I know you probably wondering why do I talk to him like this, it's because he truly understands. Lil Devin asked mommy is that little riding hood?" I answered " Yes" and left it like that.

I knew that I had to pay more attention to my son and less on foolishness!

I woke up this morning with the need to see my grand mom,

plus I haven't spend enough time with her lately. Lil Devin needs to get to know her more, after we got dress we jumped in my ride and headed straight to uncle B Kool house. When we got their he ran straight pass uncle and straight to grand moms room where he knew she would have some treats waiting for him. To her surprise he caught her off guard when he gave her a hug. She nearly jumped out of her wheel chair. Once she realized who it was she gave him a big hug back followed by a kiss. "Hi baby " and told him to reach into her bag that hung behind her wheelchair to get some goodies out the bag. She was having so much fun with him that she didn't even noticed that I was standing right behind her.

I leaned in to give her a kiss on the cheek, than sat down on the bed to do some catching up on, while lil Seem went to play with his favorite cousin Maine.

It didn't take grand mom long before she started to dig into my ass about how I never showed to do her laundry and take care of her business like I said I would. Then she said that's neither here nor their, let me get your help while I have you! Granny had no Idea that Devin and I had split up, since lil Seem had left the room I felt like this was the perfect time to fill her in now. I need to hear a world from the wise, after filling her in on every thing it left her filling heart broken. She said " I thought that I would dance at yall wedding!" Then she saw the sadness on my face and said " I believe if you love someone and set them free, if he returns to you then it's ment to be." Than she gave me a big hug with her good arm and squeeze me so tight that my air circulation was almost cut off. I couldn't hold back my tears because deep down inside the sting was still their.

After our talk I got up to take care of her cloths , I ironed enough outfit to last her for two weeks. I said "mommy I forgot to mention that I went to sign up for hair school." Then the tears started to roll down her eyes. " I'm so proud of you, you continue to strive for the best and take care of that baby because he didn't ask to come here!" "Yes mam " I said. My aunt Gina knocked on the bedroom door to ask me if I was staying for dinner? Of course my answer was yes, time went by so fast I couldn't believe it was that late.

It was to much work getting granny to come down for dinner so she allowed me to eat dinner upstairs with grand mom instead. I love my new aunt for all that she does for my grand mom, I don't have to worry about the gun shots anymore. Grand mom is living her life like its golden. I' m happy for her, when we was done I called for lil Seem to come put his coat on and say goodnight to grand mom. We gave uncle B Kool and aunt Gina a hug and kiss good night and went on our way. This lil guy fell asleep soon as he got in the car, I press the play button and listen to Mary J on my way home.

It's Friday and I'm to have some fun tonight, so I decided to take Lil Devin to his grand mom Renay house early today to spend the weekend with his aunt Reesie since they missed him. I don't know if Ms Rose remembers that I start school on Monday or not but I'll remind her before I leave. I noticed that Big Devin was not home , and the more I think about I haven't seen him since he shot me down with rejection. If he would have been there I made sure to look extra pretty just to remind him of what he had let slip away. I've been working out so hard and barely eating that I've lost so much weight . Just as I was about to leave to my surprise Devin opened the door, " Hey Trina" with his arms opened wide to receive a hug. I leaned in and gave him a quick hug trying not to seem so excited. Since he was so close to me I gave him lil Seem night bag of clothes filled with cloths that has already been iron for the week and enough PJs to last as well. I must have looked like a new women to him because he couldn't stop looking at me like I was a piece of chocolate. I decided to give him a better look and bend over in front of him to give Lil Devin a kiss before saying goodbye. I asked him to let his mom know that I would return on Wednesday to pick our son up after I was done with my first day of class.

I wanted to make him feel like he was a none factor to me ,just like he had made his son and myself feel. So I pretend to pay him no mind, jus as he was about to speak I informed him that I had to leave because some one was waiting for me in the car and I couldn't stay any longer! His responds was ok and he stood in the door to see what car I was getting into, it was a burgundy cream Burick Lasabor with tinted windows sitting on 22 inch rims. He couldn't see who was driving , lil did he know that this guy was no threat to him at all, but it sure felt good letting him think so. This was my hommy Derick he had a car for every occasion, I didn't want to drive at all today so I asked him to pick me up and also drop me off. I hope Lil Devin doesn't tell him who he is and I smiled to myself and said ooh well.

We are now at my aunt Paula house where it's about to go down at. My cousin Ricky is meeting me their. My aunt was already having her on party by herself. She was having a glass of Rum and coke on ice, with a Newport long cig. It all depends on the mood she was in if she would share a drink or not. On this day I was lucky because we had more than one drink together we had two. We drink until Ricky came , when I looked at her she looked as if she had more fun than we did, with that permanent smile placed on her face. The smell of weed was over whelming but that didn't deter me from asking if I could have some? She could barely move her lips so she just reached down in her pocket book to give me the piece that was left to smoke. Before I lit it I sked my aunt if I was ok. I never smoke in front of my aunt so I excused myself and went out in the back yard to smoke. It didn't take long before I was on cloud 9, after having those drinks on top of the weed I became stuck for a moment. When I went back in to join Ricky and aunty, I too became no company to my aunt , we both was stuck while my aunty rapped the both of our head off. Then out of no where we heard a loud sound hit the floor.

It was Ricky she had falling down o the floor, on top of it she said " Help I've falling and can't get up" we both laugh so hard. Ricky finally pulled her self up of the floor by using the chair that she had just falling out of for support to lean on. Just as she sat her butt in the chair that took her so long to get back in, the horn began to sound letting us know that our ride was now here. Making sure we heard the horn my cousin Mia yelled down the steps screaming your ride is hear. I yelled back " thanks" and we bounced. I think my friend was mad because he didn't say nothing to us but yall stink. I couldn't understand how a nigger that sold weed and other things that I'm not going to mention could be so mad.

We got their so fast that I didn't even realize we was parked in front of my apartment building, I guess it's because Ricky and I talked the whole time. I knew that I must have been drunk because I leaned over and kissed him on the cheek and said thank you to him before getting out of his car. As we walked up the steps Ricky started laughing saying " I knew yall was messing around", I slapped her on that fat ass of hers and said " stop playing with me". The first thing she said before putting her bag down was "can my friend come over for a while tonight"? then I gave her a look like I thought this was girls night! Me with my week ass said yeah but that wasn't it , and his boys too? Me " how many? " her "about 4" "Alright we minds well turn this into a party, I already have the bottles". Then Ricky said " they coming with the weed " by now I'm on the phone calling upstairs for Nelly to tell her and her sisters to come down to our lil get high party.

It didn't take long for them to show up at all, so we went on a head and got the party started. We danced laugh and talked about all of us being dumped at the same time, this time we laughed about it instead of crying. The door bell ringed and Ricky answer it , I heard her say I'll meet you in the hall. W hen they enter the apartment Ricky was all cheesing with her dude holding his hand, I guess she wanted us to know that this one was hers.LOL

They was all kinds of flavors staring at caromel to dark chocolate. They came in the door with respect, they shock our hand and introduced them selves. I had already scoped out who I wanted to chill with. His name was Bysiel he was the chocolate guy with the curly hair, the rest didn't matter any way because clearly the girls out numbered the guys so it was every women for them self. It wasn't like hooking up was part of the plan any way, the party was jumping shots was taken and the weed kept coming. We was having a ball if I didn't know any better you would have thought we knew each other for years. The Jones sisters started singing, the dudes started rapping, me and Ricky couldn't sing or rap so we just sat back and enjoyed our self.

That's when I noticed Byran checking me out, I tried to act as if I didn't noticed him noticing me We got hungry with all this drinking and smoking going on , we decided to order some pizza and chicken wings and to large sodas. One of the guys yelled out get two cokes so we can use them for our drinks, and we did. When the food got their the guy Shiz pay for the food and said this treat was on him. We all tried our best to eat as much as we could to try to consume some of the liquor we had just drink.

Byran couldn't hold it in any longer and finally gave in to his own lust. " Trina before I leave you think that I can have your phone number so I could call you Tomorrow"? I thought he looked pretty good so I gave him my number that was already written out for him. His responds was" dam you was ready " I said " I already knew you would ask for it!" and we both laugh.

It was in the morning and we decided to finally end our party at 3:00 am, we all hugged each other and said our good byes and promised that we would meet up again some time in the future.

This time instead of walking Shiz down the hall Ricky decided to just give him a kiss at the front door instead. No sooner than the door shut she fell back on it and said "boy am I tired", I said " so am I". I grabbed us a blanket we both took one side of the coach and fell fast asleep.

Soon as I walked in the building the first thing that came to my mind was high school all over again. As I scan the room I noticed the signed that hung over the receptionist desk that said Gordon Phillips. from that moment on I knew since I came here for one reason for one reason and one reason only, that was to get my certification to do what I love the most, that's doing hair.

Finally the receptionist notice me and tells me to sign in and some one will be with me in a moment. Then a older light skinned women came out with a fly Holly Barry hair cut called my name. I lift my hand to let her know that I was who she was looking for. She reached her hand out to shake mines while informing me that her name was Ms Williams, " please follow me" . We entered a small room with a few tables and chairs, " Ms Lyons I need you to take a placement test just to see how to place you and also just to fine out what you know. Then when your done we can get you started on filling out your paper work for your financial aide. She walked out an returned with a booklet and said you have 1 hour to finish your test. She left the room and the clock started, I took a deep breath and reminded myself that I could do this. I went in hard in the back of my mind all I could see was a brighter future for me and my son.

Next thing I knew was I was done with 15 minutes left on the clock, when Ms Williams came to check up on me, and realized that I was already done she said let me get the answer sheet so I can check your paper. When she was done I scored a 96, " you did great "she said and we began to fill out my papers. I was approved and received my package and also my starting date for November 4, 1992. She shook my hand and welcome me. I thanked her for her help and informed her about how excited I was about my future with their school. I couldn't believe how much my life was about to change, I took a moment to thank God and went on my way.

Chapter 11

A DATE WITH BYRAN!

My future is looking brighter for some strange reason, plus Ms Rose decided to keep Lil Devin for another week. She told me that I needed to take that time to get myself together mentally for school, and she never lied. Everything in the apartment is cleaned and put away, their's nothing left for me to do, so I decided to talk to that guy Byseal for a while on the phone to kill some time. As the phone rings I start to get butterflies and wonder if I should just hang up the phone. Then he answers " Talk to me" right off the back I began to think maybe I have the wrong number, but I go for it." Hello may I speak to Byseal?" ?" " Speaking" he said, I said this is Trina how you doing? Trying to be that same sexy dude I first met he said " hay baby what's up?" What took you so long to call me? I told him that " I was so busy getting prepared for school." We continued our conversation and we ended it with me telling him what time we would meet up tonight. He said he would be their at 9:oo o clock pm, I said "ok" and we ended our conversation.

I didn't know that he was a Muslim, I hope he don't think that he's going to convert me into one if we become a couple. So I decided to get ready for my date early, this time I decided to let my hair down and put on something a lil more comfortable. I put on a pair of black fitting tights, a see through black shirt with a black lace Bra. To finish things off I sprayed a lil of my Estee Lauder perfume on. I decided to wear my black slippers with fur on them.

Now all I had to so was set the mood, so I grabbed a bottle of Rum and placed it on ice. Then I lit my candles and had a glass myself to ease my nerves, before I knew it the door bell was ringing. I whispered into the intercom " who is it?" It's me baby, he said. As I buzzed him in I thought to myself dag now I'm his baby already. I opened the door and sat down on the coach trying not to look so dispirit. I saw him and instantly said to myself dam he looks good, he looks even better this time around. He don't smell to bad neither as he bent over to give me a hug and pulled me up and wrapped his arms around my waist. He gave me a big wet kiss on my lips like he was my man , that just came home from a hard days work.

I motioned for him to sit down on the coach while I went in the kitchen to make us a drink of Rum and coke with a slice of lemon on the side. I had to wipe my lips because I could still smell his breath on my lips. I already didn't like that about him that he was a sloppy kisser. I passed him his drink and sat down beside him so that we could talk and get to know him better, what I did find out was that he had NO JOB, no kids, no girlfriend. One more thing is that he talks too much, the more he drank the more he kept spilling the beans. I could tell he was filling it because his hands started touching places they was not invited to. I tried to let down my guard down but I couldn't get over how small his hands where. He was so handsome yet to short for me, all I kept thinking about was how I like my men a lil taller and thicker . I think that the liquor started to kick in because I stop thinking about what I

Didn't like about him and focused more on the good qualities he had. No he wasn't Devin but he gave him a run for his money in the looks department. We stop talking to listen to mint condition sing, it's getting late. This dude is full of surprises. He stood up and grab my hand so that we could slow dance together, his nature begins to rise as he gently licks the bottom of my earlobe: this time when he kissed me I kissed him back showing him how I like to be kissed. I took control. His hands slid up the back of my shirt trying to undo my bra. He slowly moved them to the front of my bra gently rubbing my now rock hard nipples. He rubbed them both at the same time. Then he began to lick then like a lollipop. It feels oh so good. I can feel my vagina throbbing,

before we went any further I stopped him because I have a son now and I need to think about before I do things to hurt him in the future. I told him to slow down. So for the rest of the night we just held each other and talked until it was time for him to go. When his cab arrived we kissed once more

And I told him to call me when he got a chance. When I shut the door I felt so proud of myself for not giving my body up so fast.

Two months later and I've learned how to apply a relaxer the proper way in hair school. I've also learned how to apply a cold wave relaxer, along with how to do a roller set. We're now learning how to do finger waves and I've come to realize that this chapter is my favorite. I am one of the top students in my class so far, and because of my love for doing waves I now get paid to do them after school. I charge $20.00 dollars a head, ai try to do at least 3 heads a day. This is what I call fast cash, my booking is becoming so big that all I think about is school trying my best to keep and A average alone with making this money to give my son a better life than I had.

I don't have a safe so I take the money that I make and place every hundred dollars and wrap it in a rubber band and place it in there for safe keeps.

On Wednesdays in hair school we have the opportunity to do each other hair for free. It seems as if every one want me to do their hair. The good thing is I make money even in school off the students. As I watch the smiles appear on my class mates face, I finally feel like I've found my calling in life. I'm moving on up like the Jefferson the girls in my apartment building is now coming to get their hair done and some of their friends. The word is spreading fast around my way from word of mouth or just by seeing a clients style. The money is flowing right now I barely have time for anybody especially that guy byseal.

Guess what word must have gotten back to Devin because we've been

Spending a lot of time together or may be I should say to hit this, I don't feel bad because he's my baby father and if I need some I minds well get it from him. We decided that we would try to work things out slowly, but he doesn't understand that his rights to answer my phone are over. He has his friends and I have mines, that's a subject that we never talk about.

What I don't like is him trying to be smart when the phone rings and he hangs up after telling my friend that he's spending time with his family and to call back! If his sex wasn't so good, I would have left him for good but I can't. One night after making love to him, we laid down in the bed just talking to each other and he came out and asked me " Trina how come your boy friend keep coming to my shop to get his hair cut by me?"

My mouth hit the floor, then he said "the next time he come to the shop its going to be a problem!" I couldn't believe what he just said because I never had a conversation about Devin with Byran. Then I realized that I never took down our family pictures and maybe that's how he knew what Devin looks like. I reinsured him that I would have a talk with him just to changed the conversation. Little did he know that I had left him alone a while ago. I didn't bother to let him know either, I figure I'd let him think their was still competition. He don't know that this pussy still belongs to him because he's the only one I feel safe with.

That all came crashing down once more the night of New Years Eve. I decided to stop by the Barbra shop with my girl friends to wish him a early Happy New Years. It was about five of us together, as I was just about to lean in to give him a kiss good bye, I noticed our car pull up in front of the shop with his niece in the passenger seat and his Bitch driving my shit like she brought it! I lost it ! I tried to snatch that hoe out of the car until Devin grabbed me and told her to pull off. My feeling was so crushed, I turned around and smacked him and called him every thing but a child of God!

I started yelling " I'm done with you ,you broke ass nigger, you can stay with that Hoe and don't ever come see me or your son any more!"

Then he had the nerve to say " Trina ,Trina we not even together any more" I said " That's not what you said to me when you was eating this pussy" Yes that's right I said it. When he looked me in the eyes and saw the hurt that I was feeling, he knew from that day on that we we're truly over!!

I couldn't go out with them after this ,so I decided to let them go ahead without me and caught a cab to my aunt Paula house. Soon as I sat in the car the cab driver asked me what was my destination? I told him 22nd and Diamond Street, Then he turned on the radio and Bryant MC Night song came on called One Last Cry! I tried to hold it back but I was hurting so bad that the tears came streaming down my face like a river of running water. I didn't realize that the driver was watching me through the mirror, I did hear him ask if I was alright? " Yes " I mumbled with my hands covering my face as I spoke. All I kept seeing was that girl driving the car that I saved my money to help buy. I reminded myself that he was a low life and has hurt me for the last time. Theirs no more coming back this time , my friends saw everything and I'm so embarrassed. I kept telling myself that if I don't stand up for something than I'll continue to keep falling for anything.

When I finally made it to my aunt house my cousin Mia held me in her arms as I cried like a baby and never did she ask me what was wrong.

I've been stacking my money for a while now, my cousin said she would take me to a friend she knows who sells used cars. I can't wait until lil kaseem see's our new car hell be so happy especially not having to stand on the corner waiting for the bus in this cold weather. The more I think about it , I can hear my grandmother voice in the back of my head saying, you can have anything you want if you believe in your self. The way things are looking up for me ,I know its my faith that's bringing me this far because I should have been lost my mind.

I reached for the phone to call my cousin Roe Roe to see what time we where leaving and to find out how much money to bring with me. She said the guy had a red and silver Renault for sell he's asking for $1500.00 so I decided to bring $1800.00 instead. She also said she'll meet me at 1:00 pm so I agree to meet her at her house at twelve and we did just that. The car was parked in the lot of Kmart on Armingo Ave, we had already looked the car over before Mr. Bill got their, I like what I was seeing and couldn't wait to go for a test drive. When he got their he handed me the keys and we went on a test drive. I don't know to much about cars but it seems to be driving pretty smooth. " I want it Mr Bill " when we got back to the parking lot I gave him the money and we both signed the papers and headed to get them signed by the notary to make things legal. After the tags and papers was transfer in my name we shock hands and the deal was done. Me being so appreciative of my cousins help I gave her $100.00 dollars for taking the time to help me find a car. We all separated up I waned to hurry home so I could get the car cleaned before my son see it. I didn't even make it all the way home when the car started to smoke actually I made it to Girard Ave where the Philadelphia Zoo is located. All I could see was white smoke ,I put the flashes on and lift the hood of the car and tried to unscrew the cap where the radiator was located and hot water shot out as I jumped back just in time.

Now I'm mad as hell I feel like I was just robbed with out a gun, I gave my hard earned money away I was thinking as I sat down in the car and began to cry. I started yelling and banging on the steering wheel asking the Lord why me and how come I can never get a brake? I started feeling sorry for myself and decided to get out the car and locked it up and walked the rest of the way home. I walked about 5 blocks until I reached 34th and Haverford Ave. When I got to the apartment I wasted no time, I searched through the yellow pages until I found a Towing company to tow my car in front of my apartment building. Then I called my friend Derrick to have him pick my son up for me and bring him to my house for me. I trust him with my son because we grew up together. I already knew he would have a lot to say to me about what had happened. So I was already for him when he got here, but instead he gave me a big hug and said if you need something give me a call. Then he high five my son and left us alone.

That next morning when I woke up I got dress and went up the street on the corner of 34 street. I introduced myself and gave him a lil information about what I experience with the car, Tony walked down the street with me and looked under the hood of the car. Tony motioned for me to turn the car on, no sooner as I did so the car started to smoke. As he shut the hood he told me that I needed to get new heads. I didn't know what he was talking about but I knew it sounded expensive. I asked " how much would he charge to fix it?" Are you ready for it he said $1000 dollars my mouth dropped. He also informed me that he would have to find me a used one or brand new set of heads and that's not included in the price he gave me. I gave him his fee of $25.00 for just taking a look, I said I'll get back with him in a couple of weeks when I'm ready to get it fix. In the mean time the car just sat in front of my apartment building while I continued to stack my cash.

My focus is on biology and chemistry in hair school ,its really getting harder and I can't afford to give up now. I never thought I had to know all of his just to do hair, it just got real for me. Now I understand why the Bible says my people perish from the lack of knowledge, I think that's how it go. I decided to stop going out with the girls for a while looking for attention and focus on my future. I'm truly learning how to love me and understand why my life has been filled with ups and downs and why I've been looking for love in all the wrong places. I'm going to wait on the Lord because the word of God clearly says that man who finds a wife finds a good thing!

At times I often hear my son father tell me that aint no man going to want you with no baby! I must admit it at times I believe its true, I sometimes wonder what life would be like if I had no baby. Then I realize that my God makes no mistakes, at times God has to remove people and things out of the way so he can take you to your destination he has prepared for you; and it may not fill good.

I try to put myself in my moms place and understand why she did the things she has done to her children, I've even thought about going to see her and trying to make things work out with her and my son, he needs to know his grand mother. I haven't seen my lil brother and lil sister in so many years, I could see them on the street and walk right pass them. Then a tear rolled down my cheek, that's when I realized that my work book paper was now wet with tears. The sound of the phone ringing had shook me out of the sadness that came over me. Now usually when I'm studding I never answer the phone but I decided to answer it this time and reached over the arm of my coach and grab the phone that was on the end table near the door.

Hello trying not to sound like I was not crying, then the strange voice on the other end of the phone Ask if they can speak to trina in a kind of deep voice. " This is she " I answered wondering whom I was speaking with. " I've been trying to catch up with you for weeks, I hope you don't mind that I got your phone number from my sister?" not once did he tell me his name. Then I asked him again whom was I speaking to? " I'm sorry This is Gina's Brother Kevon. I couldn't remember him until he explained to me that he had met me the day that my uncle moved to West Philly. He said that he was the driver." Now I remember I said the more he talked the clear his face became. I asked him " what do I owe for this phone call?

Kevon replied that he had a crush on me every since he saw me and he also said he heard that I was single and wanted to take me out on a date?

I didn't wanted to seem to be mean,but at this time I really didn't have much time to date because of school and on the weekends I spent most of my time with my son. His responds was " that he understands and didn't want to come in between our relationship. Then he asked " if I could set up a date that best worked out for me". I began to fill bad and said ok, maybe we could go out after I take my son out on Easter Sunday. I could hear the excitement in his voice as he said " ok". He then gave me his mom address on 39 and Brown street, we continue to talk for it seems like hours and to my surprise I really enjoyed our conversation and not once did he say something sexual or out of place to me, that right there was a plus sign.

He then said goodnight and even asked me to say goodnight to my son, who was not their but I said I would as I also wished him a good night. That's when I yelled "wait we didn't say what time we would meet up?" We both agreed that 8:00 would work and hung up he phone.

I could do nothing but smile as I laid the phone down on the receiver. No one has ever asked to take me out for dinner before. I couldn't wait to see him and wonder what was it about me that he liked so much that he waited this long for me! I figured that when I met him that would be one of the questions that I will ask him face to face.

I'm up extra early today preparing breakfast for my lil man and myself. I decided to go to church today with my bestfriend Kia and her son lil Bee. She's has been going to this church Freedom Baptist Church lately Baptist Church lately , located on 43 and Lancaster. It took me a while to take her up on her offer to invite me to come worship the Lord together. I felt like Easter was the perfect time to celebrate the day that our savor was resurrected from the dead. That's the real true meaning of Easter and I wanted my son to know the truth. The doors of the church opens at 10:45 and I didn't want to be late, After Lil Devin finished Breakfast we hurried up and got dress. His black dress pants ,white dress shirt, black tie and black shoes was already laid out for him. I toped him off with a black Leather jacket, after getting him dress I told him to sit still on the coach so I could get dress. I stood back and took one more look at him before leaving him and said to him " you are one handsome looking kid" and he smiled back at me because he knew that was the truth. I thank the Lord for blessing me with a healthy child and proceeded to get dress.

While he sat there on the coach like a good boy watching T V, I slid into my black dress, off black stockings and I put on a pair of black and silver hills with silver accessories. Then I unwrapped my hair letting it fall down to my shoulders put on a lil make up splash on a lil of my favorite perfume. Looked my self over in the mirror and felt happy what I had seen and walked down the hall to pick my bible up off the coffee table that was always opened on Psalms 23. I told Devin to put on his jacket as I put on my black leather blazer. We stood in front of the door with our head bowed as we took a moment to pray, and Devin said his favorite part Amen.

Devin is so happy to see so many children all dressed up like him , and most of all how pretty the girls look in their dresses. He was even more surprised when we stood at the bus stop to catch the bus. " Mommy why we catching the bus?" followed by many questions. I think he's getting use to us driving every where and now he has the case of the gas ass, sorry look at me cursing and I'm on my way to church, Lord help me!

The 31 bus came so fast and before we could even settle down good we was already there, you could hear the music from the corner of the block.

As soon as we entered the front door the ushers greeted us with a smile and welcomed us in. On our way to our seat the Pastor said let the church say Amen. The message he preached from was on Matthew 28:6. Then he finished the teaching on Jesus is the reason for the season. I felt the spirit of peace in that place and I knew from that moment on that I would return again. Then he began to call people down for prayer or to receive Jesus as their personal savor, and he also said we let go our past so we can walk into our future in other words ,if any man be in Christ he is a new creator old things are past away and all things are made new. For some strange reason I understood exactly what he was saying. Did I go down and repent , NO I'll do it next time is what I'm trying to convince myself. The offering was taken and service ended, I truly enjoyed that word in some way I feel slight different.

After church we caught the bus back to my bestfriend house were the kids had a Easter egg hunt , then we ate dinner with family as the kids played together the adults talked in the kitchen. I was kind of excited about the date I was going on later that night, so I excused myself and called me a ride to pick me and my son up so I could take him to his grand mom house for the rest of the week. when my ride got here Devin grabbed his Easter basket and we left.

My ride took me to his grand mom house and then to my house, I pad him $25.00 dollars and went in the apartment to get some rest. How can I rest when I'm so nerves my stomach is doing flips on me , I think it's the butter flies. I know how to fix that! I poured me a drink slow Gin and orange juice, not to strong just enough to calm me down; don't want to look like a drunk on the first date. I know what to do let me find my out fit, I reached over to grab the remote to my Stereo and put my girl on Mary J. The music thumping and I keep trying on outfit after outfit until I found that perfect one. I tried to keep in mind that his mom and dad would also be there and didn't want to give off the wrong vibe. So I decided to put on somethin simple a pair of brown jeans and a cream fitted shirt followed with a cream netted vest with a matching coofee hat. My hair was in a wrap hanging down to my shoulders, I didn't wear any make up just a lil lip gloss. I didn't put my shoes on until it was time to leave, I called for a cab at 7:30 on the dot. When the bell rang I reached down for my brown shoe boots and my brown leather jacket , along with my coach bag hit the lights and was out.

We arrived in no time his moms house was just up the road, I live on 34 and Haverford and she lives on 39 and Brown. The cost was $8.oo even so I gave him $10.00. Now I'm here and my legs felt so shaky as I began to walk up the steps and approach the front door. Just as I was about to knock on the door it opened , and quit frankly it startled me, after seeing that tall husky glass of chocolate milk smiling in my face it made me feel a lil relief. I could tell he liked what he sees, he leaned in a gave me a hug and whispered in my ear to say you look so beautiful. As we walked into the living room where his family was setting around talking , he began to reintroduce me to his family while reinsuring them that we have already met before. With one arm stretched toward the coach he asked me to have a seat. I said "hello" and Kevon said I forgot to say her name is Katrina.

Every thing was in the exact same place as it was when I first met them, while sitting in the company of his family it made me wish that I had the same loving family that he had. I couldn't stop looking at him as he walked away to get me a glass a ice water, I thought about how different he was from the guys that I've dated before. He looks more like a family and yet you could tell he would do any thing to protect his love ones. I checking out his gear, he has on a sweat suit the colors of the Lakers team and a fresh pair of white sneaks and from the looks of his feet it has to be about a size 12. You know what they say about big feet lol. Next thing I know I'm licking my lips and drawling like a sick puppy. Then he interrupted my thought when he reached out to hand me my water that I asked for.

We didn't stay much longer because we wanted to make the movie on time , he gave his mom a kiss goodbye and shook his dad hand and waved good bye to every one else as he helped me put on my jacket to leave. Like a choir they all said good bye Katrina at the same time. I said " nice seeing yall" and I also waved goodbye. We walked down to block to catch the 40 bus and got off at Market Street than the Frankford L down to 69 and Market. While we walked and talked I found out that he was a student at Community College for business and he also worked full time as a cook. I'm thinking that not only is he handsome and smart but he can cook too. Yes I said on the inside then I asked the million dollar question, " do you have a girl friend that I should be worried about ?" His answer was no followed by a pause, "I did have a wife and a possible daughter" my smile must have turned up side down because he said " don't worry we got a divorce because of her infidelity" I'll tell you more about that at another time, I just want to enjoy our time together Beautiful ! Then I smiled at him and that's when it happened. Pop,pop,pop was the sound of the gun shots that we heard as we got closer to the movie theater. People started running towards us and he grabbed my hand and told me to come with him in a stern voice and I did. He said I guess their is a change in my plans, lets go out to eat instead, then I interrupted him and said were going back to my place and we can watch a movie and order out. We headed back down the street an d caught the 31 bus and held hands as we talked like two high school kids. The bus finally let us off on 34 and Spring garden we walked down to 34 and Haverford where my apt building sat in the middle of the block. This is where I live as I opened the front door and he held it opened for me and the next one and the next , until we finally reached my apt door. When I turned around I caught him looking at places he shouldn't be looking at. I reached over to turn the lights on that sat on the coffee table, then I told him to have a seat, I could see him studying the pictures that was on the wall and admiring the way I fixed up my apartment. Your apartment is very nice, I put on the movie Waiting to exhale but we paid that movie no mind. I can tell that he really liked me and then he reached in and gave me a kiss on the lips, his breath was so refreshing and his teeth are so white. His kiss wasn't over barring leaving my lips soaked. I sat my hand on his lap in hopes to feel his nature by a mistake and I did. That saying was true big feet big meat. Lol We made out with each other all night but never took it any further, he wanted to wait until we got to know each other better. That night we spent 6hrs together and Kevon said he had to leave because he had to get ready for his class, before leaving he promised me that he would call me real soon. I gave him another kiss at the door before he left, I even watched him walk down the hall and he turned for the last time a wave goodbye before the door finally shut. I shut my apartment door and fell back on it wishing that our night never had to end.

It's crazy because I find myself thinking about Kevon quiet often, I haven't heard from him in about a week in a half. I tried to convenes myself that I'll see him when I see him but deep down inside I was wishing upon a star that he would call me soon. With my luck it would be easier if I had put my name in a hat and expected my name to be the name that was selected, image that!

Let me stop wishing and concentrate on this test I have to take in the morning, I need to stay focus so I turned off the TV and made flash card

On every muscle of the face and the motor points are located. Not only do we have a test I have to demonstrate how to do a facial using and naming all the manipulation skill. After studying for a while I began to practice the movements on myself and pretend that I was actually talking to my instructor.

The phone began to ring at first I tried to ignore it but it wouldn't stop so I answered it in a frustrated tone. "Hello" " Hi Babe how you been?" I had to take a deep breath because I was so excited, " Hi Boo " is what I called him in return, I'm good then I said it with out thinking " I missed you" Then he said " I miss you too and I was wondering if I could come over to see you tonight" with out hesitation I quickly said yes and offered to make dinner. The conversation ended and so did my study, I quickly washed my hands and immediately began to pull out dinner, I grabbed some chicken wings a bag of Broccoli and a couple of potatoes. My meal would consist of mash potatoes garlic broccoli and fried chicken with butter bisket.

While my food was cooking I went and slipped into something more comfortable after taking a hot shower. I put on a pair of my booty short PJs with a soft pink tank tap with matching footie. Oh lets not forget the bottle of wine on ice Taylor Port, I love it I hope he likes it. I thought to myself as I lit the candles that smelled like fresh bake apple pie.

The bell rang and I never said who is it because I had already know it was Kevon and quite frankly he was early but who cares. The smell of his cologne linger in the air after he gave me a hug and a kiss, *it felt so good to have the sent of a man in this apt again. I put my hand out for his coat to hang it in the closet. We sat down to have a couple of drinks while we waited for dinner to my surprise he liked the wine that I served. I prepared our plates and we sat in my small kitchen at my two seat table set with a candle in the center of the table. He was so impressed with me and told me that I had it goin on to be a 23year old young lady with a child, right then he came straight out and asked me if I could be his women? He went on to say that he was 27 and wanted to settle down with a good women, and he also realized that I had a son and wanted the opportunity to get to know my son. I said to him in time he'll meet him. I got up to began to wash our dishes and he stood behind me and wrapped his arms around my waist and kissed my neck and said" thank you for dinner and can I help you do anything?" My answer was "No" you can have a seat I'll be with you in a minute.*

when I was done I sat down on the couch next to him and placed my leg on top of his so he could rub my thigh. It felt so good, he then began to gently kiss my lips and proceeded to French kiss me this time and I let him. I'm trying to control myself but in actuality I want to rip his cloths off of him. Then he lifted me up off the coach and carried me to the bedroom and continued to kiss me never missing a beat. He laid me on the bed and pulled off my shorts and started kissing places I never thought he would.

That's when he took me to a place called ecstasy , my goodness I can't believe that a man so righteous could be so rugged and raw and I loved it . This man has the whole package and I wanted to keep him for myself. Then I hit that climax once more but this time I screamed out yes. And we laid there for a while in total silence , then he said that he was in love with me every since the very first day he saw me crying on the day of our move from diamond street to 63 Haverford . "I prayed for you and God sent me to you, I asked for a good women and I know it's you!" Tears began to fall because no one has ever said such a loving thing like that to me.

We both took a shower together even though I didn't give him any, he stayed over and we both got up at 7:30 in the morning because he had class in the Am and so did I. After getting dress I quickly grabbed my book bag that sat waiting for me everyday near the door and we proceeded to leave. Kevon carried my bag for me, when me made our way out the front doors of the apartment building , I showed him my car that I brought that needed work to be done before it was drivable. We continue to walk and talk until we made it to the L train station, he gave me a kiss and we parted ways.

When I got to class I could hardly concentrate from the thought of how much fun I had on last night with my new man, yes I said it we are a couple!

Months later and still things are still the same with Kevon and I. He comes over every day after work, and goes home on the weekends. Kevon still hasn't had the pleasure in meeting my son yet, I'm not the kind of mother that introduces her child to everyone she dates. Since this relationship seems to be going in the right path, I decided that its now time. I reminded Kevon once more in what he was getting involved in, that if he truly wanted to be with me that my son was part of the package. Once again he told me how he couldn't wait to meet him and looked forward to having a ready made family. Those was the words that I had hope he would say. Then he said " I would love to pay for our first day out together with your son".

Then he said " Babe while were talking can we please keep every body and their opinions out of our relationship, and also promised me that he would never put his hands on me and asked me to do the same, and one more thing; if we ever get mad with each other lets try not to argue with each other if we have to lets just walk away until things calm down a bit !"

I tried to make a joke out of the conversation as I said " ok , plus you too big for me to be trying to fight any way" He didn't find that joke to be funny.

Kevon also reached into his pocket and handed me 3 one hundred dollar bills and said to use it to help put a deposit down on my car so that I could get it fixed. I couldn't believe what he was doing for me, without me asking, I said thank you and placed it in my stash of money that I've been saving already. He don't know that the money he's been giving me every week , that I' ve been stashing that too.

If I can be honest I must say that I am really nervous about him meeting Lil Devin because he truly loves his dad. I don't think Kevon going to stand a chance, this would be the first time that he would see me with another man

Besides his dad. Plus I told him that he was now the man of our house since his dad left us.

Today is Friday and we decided to pick him up early today , I didn't stay in school all day . I decided to leave at 1:00 o clock and Kevon was off of work today so that was perfect. We called for a cab to take us to Devin grand mom house to pick him up, and then to drop us off at his favorite restaurant Pizza Hunt. When Devin got into the car Mr Kevon reach his hand over the seat and said Hi lil man I'm Mr Kevon and you are? as he strapped himself in he answered Lil Devin" and shook Mr kevons hand. Then he turned his face towards me and ask " Mommy who is this man?" I said it is mommy friend, then he cross his arms and kept staring at Kevon with this strange look on his face.

The cab finally let us out on Armingo Ave right in front of the door, Kevon paid the cab driver $ 30.00 dollars and told him to have a good night. Soon as we were seated and had placed our order Kevon took Lil Devin straight to the game area, I thought to myself now that's a smart man with a good plane. From the looks of things Kevon seems to be making progress with my son. But I don't think that I'm ready to take a chance with letting him stay the night with us tonight. It might be a lil to much for him to handle right now, I'm thinking to myself as I set back and watch them interact with each other.

Kevon spent more time with Lil Devin then he did with me then he did with me and I didn't mind. When we was finished eating dinner Kevon helped lil Devin zip up his coat and we left the waiter a $5.00 dollar tip and Kevon surprised us both by taking lil Devin up the street to Toys R Us so lil Devin could pick out a toy.

Soon as we enter the storel lil Devin went crazy, Mr Kevon said he could pick out two toys. His first selection was a wrestling man called Stone Cold Steve Alston, the second was a T Rex Dinosaur. The smile on lil Devin face was priceless. This time while we were walking out of the toy store lil Devin grabbed Mr kevon hand and said thank you so much. While we were walking down the street kevon saw a cab and flagged it down. While we all got comfortable and a flash back of the conversation that I had with lil Devin father came back to me of him saying " Who's going to want you with a son or should I say a child?"

All I could think about was I just did and oh how blessed I am, to see my new family in front of me. I silently said a prayer and thank God for answering my prayer, then I asked him to please give me a sign if this man was truly made for me?

My grand mom said you have not because you ask not, and I believe every word she says. I was so deep in my own thoughts that Kevon kind of startled me when he grabbed my hand and said Bae are you ok. " Yes" I said then he motioned for me to look at lil Devin because he was knocked out. It was almost 9:30 pm when we got in the apartment and I knew he was out for the rest of the night. Kevon carried him up stairs undressed him and put his PJs on him and placed him in his bed.

When he came back into the living room he reassure me that things would be alright. We sat down and continue to talk for a while until I became over come with tiredness. I leaned in to give Kevon a kiss an proceeded to ask him if he mind sleeping on the coach while lil Devin was here for

tonight? He said ok and grabbed himself a pillow and a Blanket and we all went to bed. I know I said he was going home but ok I lied!

We finally have enough money to get the car fix. The guy name William that works at the garage on the corner of my block said that he would charge me $100.00 dollars to rebuild my engine for me and he finally found a rebuilt engine for $500.00 dollars and as soon as I have the money he'll get started. Kevon gave him $500.00 dollars to get him started and said he'll pay the balance when the job was complete. William said that it would be done no later than 2 weeks and they shook hands and we parted ways. Kevon had to go to work from there so he kissed me and walked the opposite way so he could catch his bus on time.

As I turned to walk back to the building I couldn't help but to notice that the girls from the building was standing outside for a minute talking as I walked up. Here we go as I took a deep breath ,getting myself ready for the thousands questions. Hey yall I said as I walked up, then she said it Nell " ok girl I see you have a new friend that I notice has been coming and going for a while now" " you going to tell us his name and give us the 411 on him?" she asked No one else seems as if they really cared or not, so I just answered her with just giving her his first name, and said I couldn't stop to talk because I had something to do and kept walking. As I walked away I mumbled to myself , I'm not feeling this all in my business stuff.

Before I knew it the rumor spread fast about my new dude, I heard that some felt he didn't look better than my baby father but who cares he treats me better and that's all that matters. People or should I say girl friends that I haven't seen in a while started stopping pass just so they could see him and judge for them selves. Some liked him and some didn't , some even said that we didn't look like we was supposed to be together and the ones that think that are lonely and need to find them someone to make them happy. I'm finally at the point in my life when it doesn't matter to me what other people say nor think about me and I'm loving it.

I can't wait to tell my grand mom about him, and if she likes him than I know for sure he's ok. After we pick up the car she'll be the first person we go to see. All I need to do now is to stay focus, my grand mom always told me that misery loves company, when I was down no one ever had any advise for me and I don't think I need it now. As I sat down on the couch to gather lil Devin clothes for the following week to iron them and put each matching outfit together, I couldn't help but remind myself to speak with Devin about how he keep getting smart with Kevon when he calls. For some strange reason he feels that he has to remind Kevon that he's lil Devin father as if he doesn't already know his place. That's one thing Kevon do respect him for and that's his place as my son father. That's what I love the most about him and his family is how they treat me and my son just like we are already family.

Those weeks went by so fast when I got the phone call telling me that I could pick up my car. I was in class when William told me the car was wash and ready for a test drive. I get out of class at 4:00 and it takes me a hour to get home so I said I'll pick it up at 5:30. That gives me enough time to get the rest of the money out of my box.

I can't wait to get home is what I kept thinking as I continued to do a cold wave relaxer on my client. She could tell that I had received some good news by the way my attitude had changed. It took me all the way up until school got out to finish her hair, but it came out nice plus she gave me a $10.00 dollar tip.

I hurried and gather my things and left, walking down market street to catch the 31 bus that let me off right on the corner or my block. My apartment building seemed to be so far away the closer I got the further it felt like I had to go. Finally I've made it to my apartment and I hurry past my living room straight to the bedroom to my hiding spot to retrieve my money. I even grabbed enough to give him a tip if all went well.

Then car was all shined up even the tires, after I took the car on a test ride from my block down to 40 and Lansdown and back, I was more the happy to give him the balance plus a $20.00 tip. This time I parked my car in front of my building instead of having it towed.

It feels so good to finally have my own car with out the help of Lil Devin. I got so happy I decided to get dress and visit my old neighbor hood to see some of my old friends, plus I going to surprise Kevon and pick him up from work tonight. I didn't wait any time getting dress, I grabbed one of my favorite tape of Heavy D . I turned my volume up and headed straight to my aunt Paula house to chill with the family for a while. Every body out on the strip the boys on the block selling all kinds of dope any thing you want they got it. I gave my shout out to my homies and kept it moving.

I could always smell auntie food in the air even before you hit her front door. Her house was the very first house on the block. It took me a minute to even make it through her front door before I could stop saying hello to every one. What up Bear is all you could hear, remember this is the same house that my grand mom lived in before we moved. Aunty never locks her door so I just turned the knob and walked straight in the kitchen. Hey Bear aunty said when she realized it was me. When I sat down she automatically ask me if I wanted a lil drink. It surprised her when I said No, then proceeded to ask me how did I come here. That's when I took her to her window and showed her my new whip." That's nice Bear" and we walked back to the table to continue our conversation. " Bear is it true that you have a new boy friend?" she asked smiling from ear to ear I finally answered her question with a "Yes" . Then she said I can tell your happy because you have a special look on you that I haven't seen in a while. We both laugh and when my cousin Mia came down stairs she didn't even give me a chance to tell her about my car because she did it for me. we all laugh as Mia said I guess you going to show me which one it is mom. That's when aunty told her "don't be a smart ass". This time I didn't get up I just told her the color was silver and burgundy. She turned around and said I likey like, that was her favorite saying. I couldn't take my cousin on a test drive because she's pregnant and always sick. So I didn't stay to much longer because I had a couple more stops to make before picking Kevon up at 11:00 o clock. After going to visit some of my friends I could truly tell which one of my friends who were truly happy for me and the difference from the one who could careless from the over whelming look of jealousy that showed up on their face. Being as though I couldn't stay to long and couldn't smoke any weed with them , I think they think that I'm starting to act like I'm better than them. When the truth is I wasn't driving long enough to chance driving under the influence.

Time was moving so fast next thing I knew was I had 20 minutes to make it to Kevon job to pick him up. I said my good byes and as I walked to the car , I could feel the darts shooting me from behind as I walked away.

When ever I visit the projects I always have a silent prayer to my self as I often looked through the rear view mirror watching my child hood life fade away behind me.Thank you Jesus for blessing me, I truly know where my help comes from and re-minding myself once more to never forget where I've come from.

Beings though I had very lil time to catch him before he would catch the 43 bus. I drove up Lehigh cut over to German Town Ave because that was the fastest rout to his job as a lead chef. as I pulled up in front of his work place, their was people standing all around on the strip. It kind of reminded me of Diamond Street. As Kevon made his way through the front door all you could hear was the guys saying " alright kev, have a goodnight man or I'll catch you later" as he shook their hand good bye. Not really paying the car any attention he kept walking pass me as I sat there hoping that he would notice me. He didn't so I quickly move to plane B. Drove along side of him and pretend that I was a damsel in distress, I said " excuse me can you tell me how to get to 34 and Haverford?" When he turned around to answer me, he gave me the biggest smile then leaned in to give me a kiss. After he threw his work bag in the back seat, I got out the car and walked around to the passenger side so he could have the honor of driving us home. Yes I did say home because he spends more time with me and helping me pay my bills , I told him if he wanted to stay with me he's more than welcome. It feel so good to sit back with the one you love and just drive off with the man of my life. Even more it feels good not having to be alone at night any more and having some one to snuggle up with to help keep me worm at night.

Hurray for me it's a year in a half later , and I have completed my course in cosmetology . I went on to get my license for my manager as well. I am graduating 1 out of 4 top students in hair school. Hear I am today getting dress so I can receive my certificate. I'm so proud of my self the only sad part of it is, I have no one to stand beside me or with me to help me celebrate this special moment. Then the tears start to fall, if only my grand mom could walk ..I know she would be there with me cheering me on. While I put the final touch to my hair style, I then remember that I never told Kevon about my big day. Without even second guessing myself , I said " O well it's me as always against the world " and I grabbed my pocket book and headed out the door, happy and sad at the same dam time. I figured that I minds well drive myself to school today, because I knew that today would be a short day. The most time I would spend their would be about 3 hours. That means I'm gong to pay for parking but its ok!

As I got in the car to drive down town to school , I tried to shake off the fact of never having no one buy my side when I truly need them. I know for sure if I would have told Kevon he would have missed class to be there for me, but I didn't want to inconvenience him or to afraid of rejection. What ever it was it's to late now!

When I got to school the class had already started passing the card around to get signed. This is something each student did for each student on their graduation day. I tried to pretend not to see them as they tried their best to hide the card being passed around. I can truly say that my class mate was happy for me by the over whelming support and best wishes that was said to me. The hours passed by so fast, all you could hear, its now show time and all those who where graduating stood in the hall as they called your name out one by one. The closer they got to my name my stomach begin to hurt.

Then I heard it Katrina Lyons, that walk was to longest and yet lonely walk ever, at least I thought until I looked up and saw my girl friends face smiling back at me. Then the tears started to fall, I couldn't believe that my friends really loved me enough to take the time to stand beside me on this special day. I received Honors and my license for my Cosmetology and Managers. Then my friend Damina from my class presented me with balloons and a card filled with signature and money in it from the school. I gave everyone a hug and my friends and I left so they could take me out for lunch.

We met up at Red Lobster, we all sat at the table and order our first round of drinks and when they came my cousin Teeny gave a toast that brought tears to my eyes. The she said " girl stop all that crying" but if only she knew that I haven't felt this much love ever! Before leaving we all had one more drink and before we took a sip we promised each other , that we would always support each other no matter what. I never pulled out a Dime, and I thanked everyone for every thing and we all went our separate ways. Later that night when Kevon got off work and say the balloons in the apartment , he asked me what was they for? When I told him that was the very first time I've witness the look of heart brokenness on his face. Then he said " Babe how come you didn't tell me about it? I would have loved to be their for you?" I couldn't even say a word, then I said " I didn't think it mattered to you!" then he reashored me next time to stop thinking for him and kissed me on my forehead and said he'll take care of me later.

As I leaned in to give him a hug all I could think about how God said that " He would supply all of my needs" I finished school and had a loving family, now I need to find me a job doing what I love.

It' Monday morning and I have this strange feeling like todays going to be a good day. I'm determined to find me a job today. I grabbed my curlers , scissors, clips, combs, oil sheen, holding spray, and bagged every thing up and headed up 50 th Market where there is nothing but hair salons. I'm prepared to do a demonstration if need be, I feel comfortable in my craft and can do any style that's asked of me. I parked on 50 th Marked street and walked down to 51 and Market Street. The first shop I stopped at was Liz and Cuzin Hair Salon.

Their was this middle age Lady sitting at the reception desk listening to gospel music. Her smile was beautiful and her hair cut was on point. Hi welcome to Liz and Daughter can I help you? She asked I respond with " Hi my name is Trina and I was stopping by to see if you guys was Hiring new stylist, and if not could I fill out a application with your salon?

To my surprise the Lady said yes we are , and she began to ask me a lot of questions that I thank God that I was prepared to answer. Then she said please have a seat while I call the owner MS Liz , she has another shop down the street on the next hundred block. As I sat down I took a moment to scan the room, and I thought to myself this shop sure could use a make over. There was two other hair stylist in the shop already, from the looks of things they seem to know what they are doing. While I was waiting I all so noticed how quickly it became packed. It didn't take no time before Mrs Liz the owner walked in the door, just like a choir every one said at the same time Hi Ms Liz .

" Hello everyone" Then I over heard her asking the reception-ist " which one is she?" ok she said, as she reached her hand out to introduce herself, she motioned for me to follow her to the back of the shop. " So your interested in working at this shop?" Yes Mam I said then she proceeded to ask me if I was licensed and how long ? As I begand to explain to her how long and also what my strong points were , a young lady walked in the shop as a walk in client to be serviced but the wait would have been about another hour and Ms Liz turned to me and said today is your lucky day. I would like for your to style this young lady hair as your demo.

"Now it's time to show and prove, do you have your equip-ment with you?" Yes it's in my car I'll be right back. As I began to walk towards my car to retrieve my belongings I can't help but to feel a little nervous about doing a demo in front of people I really don't know. What I do know is that I need this job and I do know how to do some hair, so I grab my things and headed back to the shop with my head held high and my game face on pretending like this was no problem for me, shoot I'm use to pretending that's all I know.

Hi my name is Trina , how can I help you? Hi my name is Cookie and I would like to have my hair cut relaxer and curled. She said. I than motion her to meet me at the third chair in the back, then I went to gather all of my supplies at the same time trying not to let her know that I was new and using her as my demo. First I analyze her hair and scalp to make sure their wasn't any abrasions in her hair.

I also checked to see if her hair was damaged, after explaining exactly what I was doing I precede with the service. We began to make small talk with each other and I became so comfortable that I forgot that I was being watched. After applying her relaxer and shampooing her hair, I sectioned her hair into four sections followed by a guide line at the nape area. Then I preceded to cut her hair on a 0 degree and then into a 45 degree. She wanted her hair cut into a bob, and that's just what I gave her.

When I was done I sprayed her hair with a lil oil sheen and holding spray, I gave her the mirror to see her hair. The expression on her face said it all. I then began to clean up my station and place all of my equipment in my bag. Did you notice that I said my station? I know that I have the job already because I'm claiming it.

The young lady was so happy she handed me a ten dollar tip, I thanked her and she asked the receptionist if she could make a apt for next week? The room stood silent for a moment and Ms Liz said yes you can and the apt was made. When the young lady left Ms Liz and I sat down to discuss the days that I work and the days that I had off also how much of a percentage that she would take off of the money that I made each week from my pay.

We then shook hands as she welcome me into her shop as a new stylist. I turned to thank Ms Ella for her help and said good bye to my new coworkers. As I began to walk towards my car I felt like jumping up in the air and clicking my heels together and yelling thank you Jesus. I drove away thinking how my life is going to change from this day forward.

Chapter 12

GOING BACK TO CHURCH!

*K*evon is finally finish School getting his B.S.degree in Business Management and know has a knew job as the assistant director at Kearsley Nursing Home. He love working in the food business and made the decision to stay in that field, every day he has to wear a suit and tie. His schedule is every other weekend and the weekend that he's off he's also off on Monday and fridays.

I'm off on every Sunday and we have decided to attend church together at Freedom on his Sundays he's off. My life is changing for the better, I even noticed that I no longer use profanity any more. Neither do I smoke weed or hang out with the same group of friends any more. when Kevon is not at church is not at church. I attend service with my girl friend Kia, after church we take the kids out for lunch or to the park.

My love for Kevon is growing stronger every day, I'm not saying we perfect but we are striving for perfection. I finally realize that I can't make it with out the Lord on my side and I need him back in my life. I knew that when I had truly decided to change my life that I would loose a couple of my friends.

I've read it in the bible that, What is it to gain the whole world and loose your soul! That's one thing I don't want to do. I realize that I have one true friend and that's Kia. We done did every thing together except You know ! and we didn't want to neither.

Kia told me that Kevon wanted to marry me , and she was surprise that I was in agreement with her. That wasn't the first time I heard that ,my grand mom said she wanted to see me marry him and dance at my wedding.LOL

Then I told her that Ms Rose I like Kevon so much that she gave me her blessing to marry him, she said that every time Kev comes to pick lil Devin up he sits down and talks to her for a while. It's now to the point where Kevon and Big Devin shakes hands and exchange a few words with each other.

Kia and I talked so long as we sat out side on her front steps, I almost forgot about picking Kevon up from his job. It was Sunday after church me and Lil Devin was having Fun with his god brother and he asked if he could stay with his god mom , and of course she said " Yes". I gave him a kiss and said good night. Then Kia said I forgot to tell you that my apartment finally came through with the same people that your renting from, and I'll be moving around the corner from you on 36 and Spring Garden. I grabbed her a shook her so hard that she yield girl stop squeezing me so hard before you hurt my baby! I said " girl you are full of surprises, I'm the baby god mom" Then she said " I was about to ask you but you didn't give me a chance!" I leaned in and gave my best friend a hug once more and made sure I told her how much I loved her before leaving her presents.

Today is my birthday and I turned 25 years old, and I still feel like a teenager. For me today is just another day no one has never made a big deal over it and neither have I, so I've decided to go to work today an make me some money.

I forgot to mention that Boo wants to take me out tonight . He asked me to buy myself something real nice and make sure that I get off work early tonight. He doesn't no that I picked up my outfit yesterday after work I brought this two peace pants suit. The jacket is black with gold rime stone on the back of it, the pants are black slacks and I topped it off with a pair of gold shoes. You know I had to find me a small gold hand bag with the jewelry to match. When I get to work my coworker is going to give me a up due hair style, I know that I'm going to look good. As I began to get dress I can't help but think about how miserable I always feel on this day and how my parents never took the time out to say happy birthday to me or even buy me a card, but that's ok you can't miss what you never had , then I wipe the tears from my eyes and grab my car keys and head out to work.

As I place the key in the car door I remember that I already have the best gift ever my baby boy Devin. This baby brings me so much joy and when even I'm sad he always lifts me up, believe it or not he truly has a old soul and because of him I go hard in life. I truly believe that's why God gave him to me so that I would know what real love really feels like. That's why I know that this love that Kevon shows me is the real thing.

Now I'm nearly two blocks away from

my job and the closer I get to it , I can't help but thank God for my new family that I've been blessed to have at my job. To my surprise I found me a parking spot right in front of the salon, as I walked in door they all screams happy birthday to me and as I scan the room I see the food and cake followed by gift bags and of course my clients.

Me trying to hold back on my tears until I couldn't no more, and like a nut they start flowing. This time they're tears of joy so I gave in and let the river flow. My clients knew that today was a short day for me and understood that I wanted to enjoy this day, some of them agreed to let my coworkers do their hair if I didn't have enough time to get to them.

We had a ball we ate ,talked trash and had a bunch of laughs together. Meka said " Trina open up your gifts" so I did and the first gift I grabbed was the biggest bag and that was a coach bag and a wallet to match. The next gift was some perfume called Angel that smells so good, even our shampoo girl brought me a gift. Her name is Kira and she knows that I like lotion from Bath & Body , I turned around to thank everyone for my gifts and proceeded to cut the cake so I could share it with our clients, they event had some food hoagie, party wings, pizza and soda.

Time flew by so fast that I had 1hour left to finish my last client hair and make it home by 6:00 clock. I was so glad all she wanted was a wrap so that worked out fine. I was done by 5:30 pm and I had a half and hour to make it home to meet Kevon. I grabbed my gifts and the rest of my cake and hurried off.

When I opened my apartment door I saw a dozen of roses and a card with balloons on the table, the card said Happy birthday Bae please be ready at 9:00 o clock on the dot Love Kevon. I know I don't drink any more but I had a glass of wine and took my shower and relaxed up until 8:15.

I decided to get started and as I was about to put on my gold shoes Kevon walks in the door looking so good, that I almost forgot it was my birthday, lol. No but on some real stuff why is he matching what I'm wearing he leans in a give me a big kiss and says"

Happy Birthday and then he says Bae its time to go."

I reach over to grab my gold bag before leaving out the door, Boo makes sure the door is locked and we proceed down the steps and out the front door . Kevon walks in front of me to open the door for me and to let everyone know that I was behind him. Just as I reached the first step all I could see was a red carpet and balloons on both sided of the carpet that lead to a stretch Limo black. I whispered to him all somebody is going on a prom, not realizing that it was September. Then they yelled it" surprise Happy Birthday" when I looked around it was my close friends in my apartment building along with some on lookers. I couldn't believe it all was for me they gave me hugs and kisses, when they were done Kevon stood at the Limo with the door held open for me to enter. I gave him a hug and he whisper " the best is yet to come" the photographer took a couple of pictures of us and my friends before we finally pulled off, as the noise began to grow dimmer I leaned in to ask Kevon " am I dreaming?"

Boo reached over a grabbed a bottle of wine and pulled us both a glass, we had about two glasses before we reached our final destination.

We pulled up infront of the Comfort Zone Club this time we was greeted by a whole new crowd that yelled Happy Birthday to me. This time it was my family and old friends that I grew up with. I couldn't believe my sister from Hawaii who I haven't seen in years. My favorite cousin was even here, my mother even showed up. This is the best birthday ever I have never had a party before and I'm in Aww with how he worked things out. Mind you that I haven't had the pleasure of introducing my mother to him yet , so how do he even know her. Well this is not the time to figure this out, my family and friends took over the dance floor and we party like it was 1999.

The drinks was flowing and the food was so good, I didn't drink or eat much because of the excitement my mom drank my liquor for me and from the looks of it she thinks the night is her night, lol.

The Dj said it's the last call for alcohol and for the birthday girl to get in the middle of the dance floor for her last birthday dance, all who wants to dance with her form a circle around her. We dance off of Stevie Wonder song Happy Birthday to you!

The love that I felt at that moment I could never explain, how someone could love me so much and want nothing to gain but to see me smile and finally happy.

The party was over and we all said our goodnights, and on the way home I couldn't stop thanking him for such a wonderful night , I guess I had a little to much to drink because I don't remember taking off my cloths or for the most of it saying goodnight.

This dam devil wont leave me alone, the more I try to fight it the more confuse and overwhelmed I'm becoming. I can't stop feeling unworthy of the love that Kevon shows me. The thought of constantly hearing my mother calling me a dum and stupid ass bitch keeps replaying in my mind.

The sound of my son father telling me that ain't no man going to want you , with another mans baby will ever want to truly be with you! Then I began to feel how unwanted I've felt by my parents, then I ask myself how can this man love me more then the very two people that brought me into this wicket world? I know that I'm not the best looking women in the world but yet he makes me feel like I'm the only women in his world. I question myself with the thought of can I be all that this man need me to be, he asks me for nothing but to respect him as he do me.

Could it be that I just don't love him as much as he loves me? Be careful of what you ask God for because he really do answer prayer. I can clearly remember the day that I asked God to send me a good man next time who loves me more than I love him, and he did and now the enemy is making me feel like I don't deserve him.

Now I'm wondering could a man love a women as rachet as me, one with so much baggage that's to much for even me to bare.

I'm pacing back and forth on the living room floor, contemplating on how to end a relationship that I don't want any more, I'll just let him know how I feel when he walks through the door. The tears from sadness is causing a pain deep in my heart. Deep down inside I know this is not his fault. To my surprise the door began to open as his face become more clear to me, I try to wipe my eyes so I could stay focus. Then a puzzled look comes across his face, as he lie down his work bag and stare me straight in my face. Bae what's wrong as he wipes the tears from my eyes. Then I say it " Boo it's you I can't no longer hide, I'm not the one for you I try so hard to live this lie. I'm not perfect and you deserve the best, so I'm deciding for the both of us to end this train wreck

Then he wiped my tears and told me he's not going any where and spilled a little secret he felt it was time for me to hear. The tears in his eyes lead me to know that what he was about to say must be true, that he prayed to God to send him some one that he could truly be happy with and that some one is you!

Then he pulled me up from the chair and held me so tight and said " we will never have this conversation again after to-night". I continued to hold him tight and prayed that what he said was true, If I ever really loose him I don't know what I'll do.

There's a knock on the door! Who is it? Kevon yells from the kitchen which is located a few feet away from my front door. It's Anna said the voice on the other side of the door. Just as Kevon was about to open the door ,I came out the bedroom to inform him that I didn't feel like company right now. So he opened the just wide enough so he could clearly see her but she couldn't see me. " Is Trina here?" she asked "No she not but I'll tell her you stop pass". Then she asked if he knew what time she's coming back. He said " In a hour" and she finally left and Boo and I continued to do what ever it was that we was doing before she stop by.

Two hours later I decided to go upstairs to my girl friend house just to catch up on some girl stuff because I haven't seen her for a while. When I enter the room I could clearly tell that I was the topic of the conversation. The same girl who just knocked on my door was now sitting on my friend couch, that I introduced her too.

Then she had the nerve to say" Hey girl I just left your place, but you wasn't home." Then they started to smile, or should I say their was a smerk on her face. I asked her " what did she want?" In the back of my mind I was wondering when they became so close, and then again it don't matter because at the end of the day she's a grown ass women. I'm waiting , Nell being the friend that she is said " tell her!" With a shock look on her face she said " what" "when you went to visit her" Nell said. Now I'm upset and asking her " what did he do?" playing alone with them. She was taking to long ,so I turned to Nell and asked her to " tell me since you already know!" I stood their with my arms crossed right infront of Anna so I could read her face expression while Nell tell me the story. Nell said " that Kevon tried to get her to come in my apartment with him while I wasn't their." Then she told him she'll just come back later"

I pretend to be shocked over the news I just took in, and the smile on her face grew wider. That's when I turned to her once more and called her a " Liar and how I knew she was a Liar because I was there the whole time behind the door!" I heard the conversation and now I know that you're a snake in the grass and I'm glad I found out early in the game. I'm done with you!"

When she realized that she was caught she stood there with a bum ass look on her face. I told her to" never speak to me again." I left and went down stairs to tell Kevon what just happened, I was so angry that I was speaking so fast. He couldn't understand a word that I was saying, so he motioned with his hands for me to stop and catch my breath and now tell him what happened. Then he snapped and said " What and when the hell did this happened?" Then I said " today" he shouted " Bae you was standing right there" I told him to calm down because I busted her infront of everyone.

He was still mad and said " what if you wasn't here would you have believed her?" I truly didn't know because she's a very attractive women but then again all of my friends are beautiful and he never made me feel uncomfortable around any of them. " I said no Boo I just can't believe she would make a lie up like that."

Boo said " we need to get away from people like them, what do you think about us moving together and renting a house Bae, we need more room any way." I said " what about my best friend Kia who just moved closer to me on 36 and Spring Garden?" His reply was " she can come visit you but it's time for us to go."

I said "ok" in my head I was thinking wait until I tell Kia about this shit. If she was their it would have went a whole fight up in there. That's when he broke my thoughts by saying " Bae were not going to let any one brake up our relationship except ourselves," and we were both in agreement.

THE BIG QUESTION!

It's Christmas morning of the year1994 , Kevon and I are making our final preparation for Christmas dinner . We invited everyone that I'm really close to in my family, and some of his favorite family members.

I haven't been this excited about Christmas in a long time. With the help of Kevon this is going to be one of the best Christmas that lil Devin ever had. With all the preparation going on I didn't realize that I was now standing underneath the mistletoe and grab me and gave me a big kiss.

Lil Devin was standing right behind us and wanted me to give him a kiss too. He copy off every thing that Kevon does. Kevon grabs the Christmas list to make sure he had a gift for ever one that we invited. Lil Devin was the first to have a line through his name.

My baby had on his Santa hat and his cloths on for the day, he had the nerve to hand me one to wear, I did because I didn't want to spoil his fun. The music is playing and lil Devin is running back and forth playing with some of his toys.

You can clearly see that Chritmas is his favorite time of the year, just by the look on his face as we wait for our guess to appear. He shouts out Merry Christmas and a Hoe Hoe Hoe to every one who walks through the door and place a gift in their hand, and never receives one back. It didn't even matter to him just smile on their face was enough, no one never expected a gift just something to eat and drink alone with a good time. As I look around the room at all the smiling faces. I feel abit of sadness in my heart as I long to see the face of my grandmom, and my mother and father absents. I can't help but wish they was hear, the sound of laughter brings me back to grips of the event.

Every one has a plate of food starting from the babies to the ladies oh yeah and don't forget the men. Then music was so loud that we almost couldn't hear Kevon clicking a spoon on the side of a glass trying to gain our attention. Then Kevon told his helpers to grab the glasses along with the bottles of wine that he brought.

He scanned the room to make sure all of the adults had a glass filled with wine. Then he shouted out for every one attention for the last time , I was so busy talking to my lil cousin that I almost missed out on every thing until he grabbed my hand and bent down on one knee in front of me. Then he grabbed the left hand and stare me in my eyes and began to make a speech. The tears began to roll down his face as he poured out his true feelings to me in front of everyone. Then he ask me the big question." Bae will you please Marry ME!!

CPSIA information can be obtained
at www.ICGtesting.com
Printed in the USA
BVHW080218141118
533064BV00002B/101/P